U0102227

BOB DYLAN
THE LYRICS 1961–2012
鲍勃·迪伦诗歌集

慢车开来

[美]鲍勃·迪伦 著

冷霜 厄土 曹疏影 奚密 胡桑 译

GUANGXI NORMAL UNIVERSITY PRESS
广西师范大学出版社
·桂林·

MANCHE KAI LAI

LYRICS: 1961-2012
Copyright © 2016, Bob Dylan
All rights reserved.
著作权合同登记号桂图登字：20-2017-053 号

图书在版编目（CIP）数据

鲍勃·迪伦诗歌集：1961—2012. 慢车开来：汉英
对照／（美）鲍勃·迪伦著；冷霜等译. —桂林：广
西师范大学出版社，2017.6（2019.6 重印）
　书名原文：LYRICS：1961-2012
　ISBN 978-7-5495-9687-4

　Ⅰ．①鲍…　Ⅱ．①鲍…②冷…　Ⅲ．①诗集－美国－
现代－汉、英　Ⅳ．①I712.25

中国版本图书馆 CIP 数据核字（2017）第 078986 号

出　　版　广西师范大学出版社
　　　　　广西桂林市五里店路 9 号　　邮政编码：541004
网　　址：http://www.bbtpress.com
出版人：张艺兵
发　　行　广西师范大学出版社
　　　　　电话：（0773）2802178
印　　刷　山东临沂新华印刷物流集团有限责任公司印刷
　　　　　山东临沂高新技术产业开发区新华路
　　　　　邮政编码：276017
开　　本：740 mm×1 092 mm　　1/32
印　　张：8.5　　　　字数：90 千字
版　　次：2017 年 6 月第 1 版　　2019 年 6 月第 4 次
定　　价：25.00 元

目录

轨道上的血

纠结的忧伤 005

命运的简单转折 014

如今你是一个大女孩了 018

愚蠢的风 022

你走了会使我寂寞 030

与我相会在清晨 035

莉莉、罗斯玛丽和红心杰克 039

如果你看到她，问她好 049

避开风暴 051

大雨倾盆 056

附加歌词
取决于我 060

呼号蓝调 066

渴望

"飓风" 075

伊西丝 085

莫桑比克　　　　　　　　　　　　　　　　091

再来一杯咖啡（下面的溪谷）　　　　　　094

哦，姐妹　　　　　　　　　　　　　　　098

乔伊　　　　　　　　　　　　　　　　　100

杜兰戈罗曼史　　　　　　　　　　　　　109

黑钻石湾　　　　　　　　　　　　　　　116

萨拉　　　　　　　　　　　　　　　　　124

附加歌词

　　被弃的爱　　　　　　　　　　　　　129

　　"鲶鱼"　　　　　　　　　　　　　　133

　　金纺车　　　　　　　　　　　　　　138

　　丽塔·梅　　　　　　　　　　　　　140

　　七天　　　　　　　　　　　　　　　144

　　手语　　　　　　　　　　　　　　　147

　　金钱蓝调　　　　　　　　　　　　　151

街道合法

守卫换岗　　　　　　　　　　　　　　　161

新的小马　　　　　　　　　　　　　　　166

宝贝，停止哭泣　　　　　　　　　　　　170

你的爱是徒劳？　　　　　　　　　　　　174

先生（扬基佬强国传奇）　　　　　　　　177

真爱倾向于遗忘　　　　　　　　181

我们最好商量一下　　　　　　　184

今夜你在哪里？（穿过黑热之旅）　189

附加歌词
　　退伍军人症　　　　　　　　　196

慢车开来

得服务于他人　　　　　　　　　203

心爱的天使　　　　　　　　　　210

我信任你　　　　　　　　　　　215

慢车　　　　　　　　　　　　　220

要变换我的思考方式　　　　　　225

好好待我，宝贝（待别人）　　　234

人命名了所有动物　　　　　　　239

当他归来　　　　　　　　　　　244

附加歌词

　　没有义人，对，一个也没有　　247

　　烦恼在心中　　　　　　　　　251

　　你要改变　　　　　　　　　　256

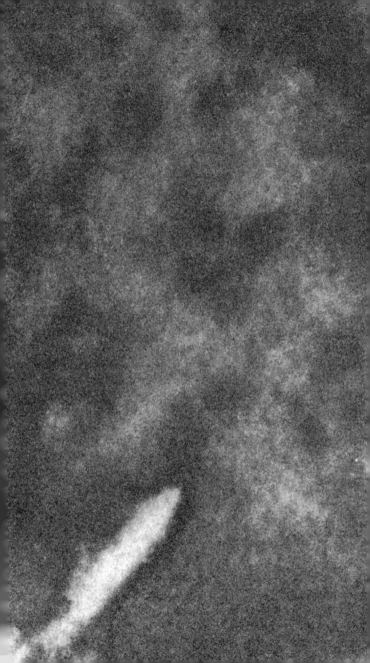

(1). <u>Early</u> 5 in the one morning, the sun was shining, he was
Lyin in bed
Wonderin' if she'd changed at all, wondering if her hair
was still red
Her folks they said their lives together sure was gonna be
rough
Never did like Mama's home-made dress, Papa's bankbook
wasn't big enough
And he was walking on the side of the road
Rain falling on his shoes
Heading out for the ol' East Coast
Lord knows he paid some dues
Tryin' tu get thr — Tangled up in BLUE

轨道上的血
Blood on the Tracks

冷霜 译

　　《轨道上的血》是鲍勃·迪伦的第十五张录音室专辑，1975 年 1 月 20 日由哥伦比亚唱片公司发行。

　　这张专辑问世后，起初所得的评价不一，但后来渐被批评家和乐迷公认为迪伦最重要的专辑之一。在《滚石》杂志评出的史上最佳五百张专辑中，《轨道上的血》名列第十六位。同时，它也是迪伦最畅销的专辑之一，曾高居《公告牌》专辑榜榜首和英国专辑排行榜第四位。此外，它还得到美国唱片工业协会的双白金唱片认证，并于 2015 年被收入"格莱美名人堂"。

　　迪伦的传记作者和很多乐评人都认为，这张专辑中的歌曲与他的个人生活有关，特别是那段与妻子萨拉（Sara Dylan）感情失和的经历。他和萨拉所生的幼子雅各布·迪伦（Jakob Dylan）便明确提到，这些歌曲就像"我父母的交谈"。故如评论所说，这是"被刻入录音带的一段对爱情自始至终最真实和最坦诚的记录"，"歌曲展示了一段触礁婚姻所引发的情感完整光谱"。但迪伦始终否认这些歌曲是自传性的，在 2004 年出版的自传《编年史：第一卷》(*Chronicles: Volume One*) 里，他声称创作灵感来自契诃夫的短篇小说。

乐评界普遍认为，这张专辑是呈现迪伦演唱与作词才华的杰出范例，体现出迪伦创造的勇气。作为一位成熟的艺术家，他并没有被自身所处的时代环境限制。它成了迪伦最好的专辑之一，乃至成了评价他作品的标尺，评论家们就常用"自《轨道上的血》以来最好的"等类似表述来称赞他日后的创作。

冷霜

纠结的忧伤 [1]

一天清晨阳光灿烂

我躺在床上

怀疑她是否已彻底变了

是否还是一头红发

她的家人说我们共同生活

一定会很艰难

他们瞧不上妈妈手织的衣服

而爸爸的存款也不够多

于是我站在了路边

动身前往东海岸

雨打在鞋子上

老天知道我已经付出了好些代价

这纠结的忧伤

我们最初相遇时她已经嫁人

很快就又离了婚

我也许帮她跳出了一个泥坑

---

1. 迪伦称这首歌用了"十年生活，两年创作"。在现场演唱中，他不时会将歌词中的第一人称置换为第三人称。

而我也为此大打出手

我们开着那辆车尽可能远走

在西部把它丢掉

在一个伤心的暗夜里分了手

彼此都觉得这样是最好

当我正要离开时

她转过身来看着我

我听见她的话音越过我的肩头

"我们哪天还会在街上重逢"

这纠结的忧伤

我在北方的大林区找到一份工作

当了一段时间的厨师

但我根本没什么兴趣

有一天我就被解雇了

于是我又游荡到新奥尔良

碰巧被招到

德拉克罗瓦[1]外边的

一个渔船上干了一阵

那段时间我都是孤身一人

昔日还没有远去

---

1. 德拉克罗瓦,美国路易斯安那州东南部的一个岛,去新奥尔良不远。

我见识过许多女人

可她从未消失在我脑海，我陷入了

这纠结的忧伤

她在一个脱衣舞酒吧上班

而我进去喝杯啤酒

我一直看着她的侧脸

在聚光灯下如此清晰

后来人们逐渐散去

我也正打算离开

她站在我椅子背后

对我说："难道我不知道你的名字？"

我小声咕哝了一下

她端详着我脸上的皱纹

我必须承认我有点不自在

当她弯下腰去系我的鞋带

这纠结的忧伤

她点燃炉火

给了我一只烟斗

"我以为你不会跟人打招呼，"她说

"你看上去好像沉默寡言"

然后她打开一本诗集

把它递给我
作者是一个十三世纪的
意大利诗人
每首诗的语言都那么真实
像燃烧的煤一样炽热
流淌在每一页上
仿佛写在我的灵魂里，由我及你
这纠结的忧伤

我和他们一起住在蒙塔古街
一个楼梯下面的地下室里
夜晚咖啡馆里放着音乐
旋律萦绕在空中
后来他开始买卖奴隶
他的内心里有些东西死了
她不得不卖掉她拥有的一切
并把内心封冻起来
当最后一切都彻底完蛋
我开始变得孤僻
我唯一知道如何去做的
是像鸟一样一直一直地飞
这纠结的忧伤

所以现在我重新回来

无论如何我得回到她身边

我们曾经认识的所有人

如今对我都是一个幻象

他们有的是数学家

有的是木匠的老婆

我不知道这一切是如何开始的

不知道他们都是如何度过人生

然而我，我仍然在路上

前往另一个酒吧

我们总是有着同样的感受

只是我们看待的角度不同

这纠结的忧伤

Tangled Up in Blue

Early one mornin' the sun was shinin'
I was layin' in bed
Wond'rin' if she'd changed at all
If her hair was still red
Her folks they said our lives together
Sure was gonna be rough
They never did like Mama's homemade dress
Papa's bankbook wasn't big enough
And I was standin' on the side of the road
Rain fallin' on my shoes
Heading out for the East Coast
Lord knows I've paid some dues gettin' through
Tangled up in blue

She was married when we first met
Soon to be divorced
I helped her out of a jam, I guess
But I used a little too much force
We drove that car as far as we could
Abandoned it out West
Split up on a dark sad night
Both agreeing it was best
She turned around to look at me
As I was walkin' away
I heard her say over my shoulder
"We'll meet again someday on the avenue"
Tangled up in blue

I had a job in the great north woods

Working as a cook for a spell
But I never did like it all that much
And one day the ax just fell
So I drifted down to New Orleans
Where I happened to be employed
Workin' for a while on a fishin' boat
Right outside of Delacroix
But all the while I was alone
The past was close behind
I seen a lot of women
But she never escaped my mind, and I just grew
Tangled up in blue

She was workin' in a topless place
And I stopped in for a beer
I just kept lookin' at the side of her face
In the spotlight so clear
And later on as the crowd thinned out
I's just about to do the same
She was standing there in back of my chair
Said to me, "Don't I know your name?"
I muttered somethin' underneath my breath
She studied the lines on my face
I must admit I felt a little uneasy
When she bent down to tie the laces of my shoe
Tangled up in blue

She lit a burner on the stove
And offered me a pipe
"I thought you'd never say hello," she said
"You look like the silent type"
Then she opened up a book of poems
And handed it to me

Written by an Italian poet
From the thirteenth century
And every one of them words rang true
And glowed like burnin' coal
Pourin' off of every page
Like it was written in my soul from me to you
Tangled up in blue

I lived with them on Montague Street
In a basement down the stairs
There was music in the cafés at night
And revolution in the air
Then he started into dealing with slaves
And something inside of him died
She had to sell everything she owned
And froze up inside
And when finally the bottom fell out
I became withdrawn
The only thing I knew how to do
Was to keep on keepin' on like a bird that flew
Tangled up in blue

So now I'm goin' back again
I got to get to her somehow
All the people we used to know
They're an illusion to me now
Some are mathematicians
Some are carpenters' wives
Don't know how it all got started
I don't know what they're doin' with their lives
But me, I'm still on the road
Headin' for another joint
We always did feel the same

We just saw it from a different point of view
Tangled up in blue

命运的简单转折 [1]

他们一起坐在公园里

黄昏的天空逐渐变暗

她看着他，他觉得有颗火星刺痛了骨头

那一刻他感到孤单，多希望还能重新开始

并提防命运的简单转折

他们沿着旧运河一直走

有些茫然，我清楚地记得

而后停下来走进一家霓虹灯炽亮的陌生旅馆

他感到夜晚的热浪迎面袭来，像一列货车

呼啸，带着命运的简单转折

一支萨克斯风吹奏在很远的地方

此时她正穿过走廊

当他醒来，光线已刺透了破旧的窗帘

她往门边盲人的碗里丢了枚硬币

---

1. 歌名原为《第四街情事》(*4th Street Affair*)，迪伦在 20 世纪 60 年代初，
曾住在纽约第四街。迪伦在 1978 年的东京演唱会上提到，"这是一个简单的
爱情故事，发生在我身上"。英国传记作家克林顿·黑林（Clinton Heylin）
认为这是关于迪伦前女友苏西·罗托洛（Suze Rotolo）的。

抛之脑后的是命运的简单转折

他醒来，房间空空荡荡
到处都找不到她
他对自己说他不在乎，把窗子大开
内心却感到一种说不出来的空虚
带来它的，是命运的简单转折

他听见了钟的滴答
然后带着一只饶舌的鹦鹉上路
去所有水手登岸的码头追寻她
也许她还会认出他来，而他得再一次
等多久，因为命运的简单转折

人们对我说这是罪过
当你内心的思考和感受太多
我仍然相信她和我是一对，可我弄丢了戒指
她出生在春天，而我出生得太迟
要怪就怪这命运的简单转折

Simple Twist of Fate

They sat together in the park
As the evening sky grew dark
She looked at him and he felt a spark tingle to his bones
'Twas then he felt alone and wished that he'd gone straight
And watched out for a simple twist of fate

They walked along by the old canal
A little confused, I remember well
And stopped into a strange hotel with a neon burnin' bright
He felt the heat of the night hit him like a freight train
Moving with a simple twist of fate

A saxophone someplace far off played
As she was walkin' by the arcade
As the light bust through a beat-up shade where he was
   wakin' up
She dropped a coin into the cup of a blind man at the gate
And forgot about a simple twist of fate

He woke up, the room was bare
He didn't see her anywhere
He told himself he didn't care, pushed the window open wide
Felt an emptiness inside to which he just could not relate
Brought on by a simple twist of fate

He hears the ticking of the clocks
And walks along with a parrot that talks
Hunts her down by the waterfront docks where the sailors
   all come in

Maybe she'll pick him out again, how long must he wait
Once more for a simple twist of fate

People tell me it's a sin
To know and feel too much within
I still believe she was my twin, but I lost the ring
She was born in spring, but I was born too late
Blame it on a simple twist of fate

如今你是一个大女孩了

我们的交谈简短而愉快
差一点就把我迷住
我又回到了雨中，哦哦
你却站在干的地面
不知怎么你做到了
如今你是一个大女孩了

远处篱笆上立着的鸟
自费为我唱它的歌
我就像是那只鸟，哦哦
只是为你而唱着
我希望你能听见
听见我带泪唱着

时光是架喷气式飞机，飞得太快
哦，多么可惜，如果我们共同拥有的无法延续
我可以改变，我发誓，哦哦
只要你能做的
我都能够做到
你也可以这样

爱是如此简单，就像常言所说
这你一直都明白，而我如今才懂得
哦，我知道在哪儿能找到你，哦哦
在某人的房间里
这是我必须付出的代价
你完全是一个大女孩了

都知道天气的变化会很极端
可生活猝然被改变是什么感觉？
我要疯了，哦哦
痛苦周而复始
像螺丝锥钻着我的心
自从我们分手以后

You're a Big Girl Now

Our conversation was short and sweet
It nearly swept me off-a my feet
And I'm back in the rain, oh, oh
And you are on dry land
You made it there somehow
You're a big girl now

Bird on the horizon, sittin' on a fence
He's singin' his song for me at his own expense
And I'm just like that bird, oh, oh
Singin' just for you
I hope that you can hear
Hear me singin' through these tears

Time is a jet plane, it moves too fast
Oh, but what a shame if all we've shared can't last
I can change, I swear, oh, oh
See what you can do
I can make it through
You can make it too

Love is so simple, to quote a phrase
You've known it all the time, I'm learnin' it these days
Oh, I know where I can find you, oh, oh
In somebody's room
It's a price I have to pay
You're a big girl all the way

A change in the weather is known to be extreme

But what's the sense of changing horses in midstream?
I'm going out of my mind, oh, oh
With a pain that stops and starts
Like a corkscrew to my heart
Ever since we've been apart

愚蠢的风

有人要找我的茬儿，在报上编我的瞎话
我希望他们收手，但也只能这么想想
他们说我杀了格雷，带他老婆去了意大利
她继承了一百万元遗产，死后就都归了我
我要有这么好运气那不是我的错

人们一直看得到我，只是忘了该怎么做
脑子里满是些概念、想象和扭曲的事实
就连你，昨天也问我钱在哪儿
我不敢相信这么多年，你对我的了解不过尔尔
亲爱的女士

愚蠢的风啊，每当你动嘴时就刮起来
顺着后街朝南吹
愚蠢的风啊，每当你启齿时就刮起来
你是个傻瓜，宝贝
你还知道怎么呼吸，这可真是个奇迹

我碰上一个算命先生，告诉我小心被雷击
我已太久得不到安宁，忘了那是什么滋味

一个孤独的士兵挂在十字架上，货车门里浓烟滚滚
你不明白，你认为不可能做到，最终他赢了战争
在输掉了每一场战斗之后

我在路边醒来，幻想着事情有时的样子
幻象中你的栗色母马洞穿我的脑袋让我眼冒金星
你伤害了我最爱的那些人，还用谎言掩盖真相
总有一天你会掉进阴沟，苍蝇嗡鸣在你眼旁
鲜血溅在你的鞍上

愚蠢的风啊，吹过你坟上的野花
吹过你房间的窗帘
愚蠢的风啊，每当你启齿时就刮起来
你是个傻瓜，宝贝
你还知道怎么呼吸，这可真是个奇迹

是重力羁绊着我们，而命运又使我们分离
你驯服了我笼中的狮子，却不足以使我改变心意
现在一切都有些颠倒，事实上车轮已停转
好成了坏，坏成了好，你会发现当你到达山顶时
你正处在谷底

我在典礼上注意到，你堕落的行为已使你迷失

你的样子陌生，说的话也变了，你不再看着我的双眼
在第七天牧师穿着黑衣冷漠地坐着，当大楼燃烧
我在车踏板上等你，在柏树边，当春天慢慢
变成了秋天

愚蠢的风啊，绕着我的头骨转着圈刮
从大古力水坝[1]刮到国会大厦
愚蠢的风啊，每当你启齿时就刮起来
你是个傻瓜，宝贝
你还知道怎么呼吸，这可真是个奇迹

我再也感觉不到你了，甚至无法去碰你读过的书
每次缓缓经过你的门前，我多希望那不是我
沿着大道，沿着小径，沿着心醉神迷之路
在繁星下我跟随着你，紧追着我的是你的记忆
和你极致的美丽

这是我最后一次被欺骗，现在我终于自由
在隔开你我的分界线上，我向那咆哮的野兽吻别
你永远不会懂得我受的伤和我克服的痛苦

---

1. 大古力水坝，位于美国华盛顿州哥伦比亚河上，为美国最大的发电和灌溉
两用水坝。"大古力"意为巨大的石槽。

我也同样永远不会懂得你，你的圣洁和你那种爱

而这让我多么难过

愚蠢的风啊，吹过我们外衣的纽扣

吹过我们写下的信

愚蠢的风啊，吹过我们架上的灰尘

我们都是傻瓜，宝贝

我们还能养活自己，这可真是个奇迹

Idiot Wind

Someone's got it in for me, they're planting stories in the
press
Whoever it is I wish they'd cut it out but when they will I
can only guess
They say I shot a man named Gray and took his wife to Italy
She inherited a million bucks and when she died it came to
me
I can't help it if I'm lucky

People see me all the time and they just can't remember
how to act
Their minds are filled with big ideas, images and distorted
facts
Even you, yesterday you had to ask me where it was at
I couldn't believe after all these years, you didn't know me
better than that
Sweet lady

Idiot wind, blowing every time you move your mouth
Blowing down the backroads headin' south
Idiot wind, blowing every time you move your teeth
You're an idiot, babe
It's a wonder that you still know how to breathe

I ran into the fortune-teller, who said beware of lightning
that might strike
I haven't known peace and quiet for so long I can't remember
what it's like

There's a lone soldier on the cross, smoke pourin' out of a
  boxcar door
You didn't know it, you didn't think it could be done, in
  the final end he won the wars
After losin' every battle

I woke up on the roadside, daydreamin' 'bout the way things
  sometimes are
Visions of your chestnut mare shoot through my head and
  are makin' me see stars
You hurt the ones that I love best and cover up the truth
  with lies
One day you'll be in the ditch, flies buzzin' around your
  eyes
Blood on your saddle

Idiot wind, blowing through the flowers on your tomb
Blowing through the curtains in your room
Idiot wind, blowing every time you move your teeth
You're an idiot, babe
It's a wonder that you still know how to breathe

It was gravity which pulled us down and destiny which
  broke us apart
You tamed the lion in my cage but it just wasn't enough to
  change my heart
Now everything's a little upside down, as a matter of fact
  the wheels have stopped
What's good is bad, what's bad is good, you'll find out when
  you reach the top
You're on the bottom

I noticed at the ceremony, your corrupt ways had finally
    made you blind
I can't remember your face anymore, your mouth has
    changed, your eyes don't look into mine
The priest wore black on the seventh day and sat stone-faced
    while the building burned
I waited for you on the running boards, near the cypress
    trees, while the springtime turned
Slowly into autumn

Idiot wind, blowing like a circle around my skull
From the Grand Coulee Dam to the Capitol
Idiot wind, blowing every time you move your teeth
You're an idiot, babe
It's a wonder that you still know how to breathe

I can't feel you anymore, I can't even touch the books
    you've read
Every time I crawl past your door, I been wishin' I was
    somebody else instead
Down the highway, down the tracks, down the road to
    ecstasy
I followed you beneath the stars, hounded by your memory
And all your ragin' glory

I been double-crossed now for the very last time and now I'm
    finally free
I kissed goodbye the howling beast on the borderline which
    separated you from me
You'll never know the hurt I suffered nor the pain I rise
    above
And I'll never know the same about you, your holiness or
    your kind of love

And it makes me feel so sorry

Idiot wind, blowing through the buttons of our coats
Blowing through the letters that we wrote
Idiot wind, blowing through the dust upon our shelves
We're idiots, babe
It's a wonder we can even feed ourselves

你走了会使我寂寞

我看着爱从我门口走过
它从来没有这么接近
没有这么简单这么从容
不再在黑暗中久久地摸索
当有些事情不对了它就是错的
你走了会使我寂寞

龙形的云朵高高地飘浮
我只知道无忧无虑的爱
它总是从下面打击我
这一次它更加精准
如此直接，正中要害
你走了会使我寂寞

紫色的三叶草，安妮王后的花边 [1]
深红色的头发环着你的脸
你会使我哭泣如果你不知道

---

1. 安妮王后的花边，在美国英语里是野胡萝卜的别称，通常开白色或淡黄色的花。

我曾经在想什么我全都忘了
你可能把我宠坏了，亲爱的
你走了会使我寂寞

野花在山边疯狂地开放
蟋蟀们反复而单调地吟唱
蓝色的河水慢吞吞地流淌
我可以永远陪伴你而忘记时光

事情已经悲哀地结束
所有关系都很糟糕
我们一度就像魏尔伦和兰波
可我已无法拿所有那些情形
和这次恋情比较
你走了会使我寂寞

你会让我怀疑我都在做些什么
失去了你，远远地落在后面
你会让我怀疑我都在说些什么
你会让我和自己好好地谈谈

我要去找你到老火奴鲁鲁

到旧金山和阿什塔比拉 [1]

我知道你只是不得不离开我

但我会看到你，在天上

在高高的草丛，也在我爱的每一个人之中

你走了会使我寂寞

---

1. 阿什塔比拉，美国俄亥俄州东北部港口。

You're Gonna Make Me Lonesome When You Go

I've seen love go by my door
It's never been this close before
Never been so easy or so slow
Been shooting in the dark too long
When somethin's not right it's wrong
Yer gonna make me lonesome when you go

Dragon clouds so high above
I've only known careless love
It's always hit me from below
This time around it's more correct
Right on target, so direct
Yer gonna make me lonesome when you go

Purple clover, Queen Anne's lace
Crimson hair across your face
You could make me cry if you don't know
Can't remember what I was thinkin' of
You might be spoilin' me too much, love
Yer gonna make me lonesome when you go

Flowers on the hillside, bloomin' crazy
Crickets talkin' back and forth in rhyme
Blue river runnin' slow and lazy
I could stay with you forever and never realize the time

Situations have ended sad
Relationships have all been bad

Mine've been like Verlaine's and Rimbaud
But there's no way I can compare
All those scenes to this affair
Yer gonna make me lonesome when you go

Yer gonna make me wonder what I'm doin'
Stayin' far behind without you
Yer gonna make me wonder what I'm sayin'
Yer gonna make me give myself a good talkin' to

I'll look for you in old Honolulu
San Francisco, Ashtabula
Yer gonna have to leave me now, I know
But I'll see you in the sky above
In the tall grass, in the ones I love
Yer gonna make me lonesome when you go

与我相会在清晨

与我相会在清晨，56 街和瓦巴莎 [1]
与我相会在清晨，56 街和瓦巴莎
亲爱的，我们会在堪萨斯
当雪开始融化

他们说破晓之前是最黑暗的
他们说破晓之前是最黑暗的
但你不会知道
你走后的每一天都是黑暗的

小公鸡咯咯叫，它心里一定有什么事
小公鸡咯咯叫，它心里一定有什么事
唉，我觉得我就像这只公鸡
亲爱的，你对我可真狠心

鸟儿们低飞，亲爱的我无依无靠
唉，鸟儿们低飞，亲爱的我无依无靠
唉，现在我没有任何人可相配

---

1. 瓦巴莎，美国明尼苏达州的一个县，61 号公路经过此地。

车站的门也关上了

唉，我翻过了带刺的铁丝，感觉冰雹又落了下来
唉，我翻过了带刺的铁丝，感觉冰雹又落了下来
唉，你知道我甚至甩掉了猎犬
亲爱的，你知道我赢得过你的爱

看那太阳像船一般下沉
看那太阳像船一般下沉
那不就像我的心吗宝贝
当你亲吻我的嘴唇？

Meet Me in the Morning

Meet me in the morning, 56th and Wabasha
Meet me in the morning, 56th and Wabasha
Honey, we could be in Kansas
By time the snow begins to thaw

They say the darkest hour is right before the dawn
They say the darkest hour is right before the dawn
But you wouldn't know it by me
Every day's been darkness since you been gone

Little rooster crowin', there must be something on his mind
Little rooster crowin', there must be something on his mind
Well, I feel just like that rooster
Honey, ya treat me so unkind

The birds are flyin' low babe, honey I feel so exposed
Well, the birds are flyin' low babe, honey I feel so exposed
Well now, I ain't got any matches
And the station doors are closed

Well, I struggled through barbed wire, felt the hail fall from
    above
Well, I struggled through barbed wire, felt the hail fall from
    above
Well, you know I even outran the hound dogs
Honey, you know I've earned your love

Look at the sun sinkin' like a ship
Look at the sun sinkin' like a ship

Ain't that just like my heart, babe
When you kissed my lips?

莉莉、罗斯玛丽和红心杰克

欢宴结束，小伙子们正打算去干一票
卡巴莱酒吧安静下来，只有墙上钻头在响
宵禁解除，轮盘赌已打烊
任何有理智的人都已离开小镇
他站在门口，看起来就像红心杰克

他穿过装有镜子的房间，说："给每个人都准备好了"
每个人都转头看看他，然后又开始做之前在做的事
接着他走向一个陌生人，咧嘴笑着问
"朋友，可否告诉我演出几点开始？"
然后他走进角落，低下头就像红心杰克

后台的姑娘们在楼梯旁玩着梭哈
莉莉有两张王后，正在等第三张来配这一对
街上满是人，窗户大开
微风吹拂，在屋里也能感觉到
莉莉又叫了一次注，抽到了红心杰克

精明过人的大吉姆，拥有镇上唯一的钻石矿
走进来时总是派头十足

带着保镖，掂着银杖，头发纹丝不乱

他应有尽有，挥霍无度

但他的保镖和银杖都比不上红心杰克

罗斯玛丽梳好头发，坐着马车来到镇上

翩翩然穿过侧门，像个无冕的王后

她忽闪着假睫毛，在他耳边低语

"抱歉，亲爱的，我来晚了。"可他像没听到

他正呆呆地盯着红心杰克

"那张脸我以前见过，"大吉姆心想

"可能在墨西哥，或在谁架子上的照片里"

这时候人群开始跺脚，灯光变暗

在房间的黑暗中只有吉姆和他

凝视着那只蝴蝶，她刚抽到红心杰克

莉莉是个公主，皮肤白皙可爱如孩童

她做着不得不做的一切，笑起来光彩熠熠

她从一个破碎的家庭逃离，与三教九流的男人

去过各种地方，有过许多风流韵事

但她从没遇到过哪个人像红心杰克

惯判绞刑的法官不声不响地进来，又吃又喝

钻头在墙上一直响，却似乎谁都没注意
谁都知道莉莉有吉姆给的戒指
没有什么会破坏莉莉与国王之间的关系
不，不会有什么，也许除了红心杰克

罗斯玛丽开始酗酒，一边看着她在小刀上映出的影子
她厌倦了被人关注，厌倦了扮演大吉姆老婆的角色
她做过许多糟糕的事，有次甚至尝试自杀
她只盼着在死之前做件善事
她注视着未来，寄希望于红心杰克

莉莉洗了脸，脱下衣服，把它们藏起来
"你的运气都用光了？"她笑，"我想你一定知道会有这天
小心别碰这墙，油漆还没干
真高兴看到你还活着，你看着像个圣徒"
脚步声沿着走廊，奔向红心杰克

后台经理绕着椅子踱步
"发生了些奇怪的事，"他说，"我能隐约地感觉到"
他去找法官，法官却酩酊大醉
当主角一身僧侣装扮匆匆经过
没有任何地方的演员比得上红心杰克

莉莉的双臂环绕着她深爱的男人

忘记了她无法忍受的那个追求者的一切

"我如此想念你。"她对他说，他觉得她情真意切

但门外却让他感到嫉妒和恐惧

这是人生中又一个夜晚，属于红心杰克

没人清楚状况，但他们说事情发生得很快

更衣室的门突然打开，一支冰冷的左轮手枪咔嗒一响

大吉姆站在那里，这倒不算意外

罗斯玛丽就在他旁边，目光很平静

她跟着大吉姆，心却偏向了红心杰克

隔了两个门面，小伙子们终于破墙而入

洗劫了银行保险箱，据说偷走了一大笔钱

黑暗里，他们在河床边上等待

有个人在镇上还有事要办

而他们不可能走得更远，要没有红心杰克

第二天是绞刑日，天气阴沉暗黑

大吉姆躺着，身上盖着布，被一把小刀从背后杀死

罗斯玛丽上了绞架，眼睛一眨都不眨

法官很清醒，他没有喝酒

唯一在场而消失的人是红心杰克

如今卡巴莱酒吧空空荡荡，告示写着："停业维修"

莉莉也已洗手不干

她想着她很少见到的父亲

想着罗斯玛丽，还想到法律

但她想得最多的还是红心杰克

Lily, Rosemary and the Jack of Hearts

The festival was over, the boys were all plannin' for a fall
The cabaret was quiet except for the drillin' in the wall
The curfew had been lifted and the gamblin' wheel shut
down
Anyone with any sense had already left town
He was standin' in the doorway lookin' like the Jack of
Hearts

He moved across the mirrored room, "Set it up for
everyone," he said
Then everyone commenced to do what they were doin'
before he turned their heads
Then he walked up to a stranger and he asked him with
a grin
"Could you kindly tell me, friend, what time the show
begins?"
Then he moved into the corner, face down like the Jack of
Hearts

Backstage the girls were playin' five-card stud by the stairs
Lily had two queens, she was hopin' for a third to match her
pair
Outside the streets were fillin' up, the window was open
wide
A gentle breeze was blowin', you could feel it from inside
Lily called another bet and drew up the Jack of Hearts

Big Jim was no one's fool, he owned the town's only
diamond mine

044

He made his usual entrance lookin' so dandy and so fine
With his bodyguards and silver cane and every hair in place
He took whatever he wanted to and he laid it all to waste
But his bodyguards and silver cane were no match for the
   Jack of Hearts

Rosemary combed her hair and took a carriage into town
She slipped in through the side door lookin' like a queen
   without a crown
She fluttered her false eyelashes and whispered in his ear
"Sorry, darlin', that I'm late," but he didn't seem to hear
He was starin' into space over at the Jack of Hearts

"I know I've seen that face before," Big Jim was thinkin' to
   himself
"Maybe down in Mexico or a picture up on somebody's
   shelf"
But then the crowd began to stamp their feet and the
   houselights did dim
And in the darkness of the room there was only Jim and him
Starin' at the butterfly who just drew the Jack of Hearts

Lily was a princess, she was fair-skinned and precious as
   a child
She did whatever she had to do, she had that certain flash
   every time she smiled
She'd come away from a broken home, had lots of strange
   affairs
With men in every walk of life which took her everywhere
But she'd never met anyone quite like the Jack of Hearts

The hangin' judge came in unnoticed and was being wined
   and dined

The drillin' in the wall kept up but no one seemed to pay it any mind
It was known all around that Lily had Jim's ring
And nothing would ever come between Lily and the king
No, nothin' ever would except maybe the Jack of Hearts

Rosemary started drinkin' hard and seein' her reflection in the knife
She was tired of the attention, tired of playin' the role of Big Jim's wife
She had done a lot of bad things, even once tried suicide
Was lookin' to do just one good deed before she died
She was gazin' to the future, riding on the Jack of Hearts

Lily washed her face, took her dress off and buried it away
"Has your luck run out?" she laughed at him, "Well, I guess you must have known it would someday
Be careful not to touch the wall, there's a brand-new coat of paint
I'm glad to see you're still alive, you're lookin' like a saint"
Down the hallway footsteps were comin' for the Jack of Hearts

The backstage manager was pacing all around by his chair
"There's something funny going on," he said, "I can just feel it in the air"
He went to get the hangin' judge, but the hangin' judge was drunk
As the leading actor hurried by in the costume of a monk
There was no actor anywhere better than the Jack of Hearts

Lily's arms were locked around the man that she dearly loved to touch

She forgot all about the man she couldn't stand who
hounded her so much
"I've missed you so," she said to him, and he felt she was
sincere
But just beyond the door he felt jealousy and fear
Just another night in the life of the Jack of Hearts

No one knew the circumstance but they say that it
happened pretty quick
The door to the dressing room burst open and a cold
revolver clicked
And Big Jim was standin' there, ya couldn't say surprised
Rosemary right beside him, steady in her eyes
She was with Big Jim but she was leanin' to the Jack of
Hearts

Two doors down the boys finally made it through the wall
And cleaned out the bank safe, it's said that they got off
with quite a haul
In the darkness by the riverbed they waited on the ground
For one more member who had business back in town
But they couldn't go no further without the Jack of Hearts

The next day was hangin' day, the sky was overcast and
black
Big Jim lay covered up, killed by a penknife in the back
And Rosemary on the gallows, she didn't even blink
The hangin' judge was sober, he hadn't had a drink
The only person on the scene missin' was the Jack of Hearts

The cabaret was empty now, a sign said, "Closed for repair"
Lily had already taken all of the dye out of her hair
She was thinkin' 'bout her father, who she very rarely saw

Thinkin' 'bout Rosemary and thinkin' about the law
But most of all she was thinkin' 'bout the Jack of Hearts

如果你看到她，问她好

如果你看到她，问她好，她可能在丹吉尔[1]
这座城市在海的那边，离这里不算太远
跟她说我一切都好，虽然事情进展有些慢
她可能以为我忘了她，别告诉她并非如此

我们大吵过一架，情侣们时常会这样
但想想她那晚怎么离开的，那真是把我伤透了
那种情形让我痛彻骨髓
我想找个人取代她，我不愿孤身一人

我四方游走，见到过许多人
到处都会听到她的名字
我始终无法释怀，只能装没听见
她的双眼湛蓝，头发也湛蓝，她的肌肤如此娇柔

夕阳落下，黄月升起，我重温往事
每一幕都记在心底，而它们都已飞逝
假如她回到这里，我真希望她不会
告诉她可以来看看我，我要么在这儿要么不在

---

1. 丹吉尔，摩洛哥北部城市，位于直布罗陀海峡的丹吉尔湾口。

If You See Her, Say Hello

If you see her, say hello, she might be in Tangier
It's the city 'cross the water, not too far from here
Say for me that I'm all right though things are kind of slow
She might think that I've forgotten her. Don't tell her it
  isn't so

We had a falling-out, like lovers sometimes do
But to think of how she left that night, it hurts me through
  and through
And though our situation pierced me to the bone
I got to find someone to take her place. I don't like to be
  alone

I see a lot of people as I make the rounds
And I hear her name here and there as I go from town to
  town
And I've never gotten used to it, I've just learned to turn it
  off
Her eyes were blue, her hair was too, her skin so sweet and
  soft

Sundown, yellow moon, I replay the past
I know every scene by heart, they all went by so fast
If she's passin' back this way, and I sure hope she don't
Tell her she can look me up. I'll either be here or I won't

避开风暴 [1]

那是另一种人生，全是由血汗构成
邪恶变成美德，道路遍布泥泞
我从荒野中到来，一个散了架的生命
"进来吧，"她说，"我会让你避开风暴"

如果我能再来一次，你放心
我会为她全力以赴，我保证
死亡牢牢盯着这世间，而人们拼命以求生存
"进来吧，"她说，"我会让你避开风暴"

我们之间未交一言，不涉及什么风险
所有事情都尚待明确
试想有一个地方，始终安全而温暖
"进来吧，"她说，"我会让你避开风暴"

我精疲力竭，而被冰雹痛击

1.《旧约·以赛亚书》32:2："必有一人像避风所和避暴雨的隐密处，又像河流在干旱之地，像大磐石的影子在疲乏之地。"注释凡涉《圣经》处，译文一律引自和合本，供大致的参照；《圣经》中屡见者，一般仅引一条。

在灌木丛里中毒，在小路上奄奄一息
像只被捕猎的鳄鱼，被踩躏于玉米地
"进来吧，"她说，"我会让你避开风暴"

突然我转过身来而她站在那里
手腕戴着银镯，发间缀着花朵
她如此优雅地走向我，取下我的荆冠
"进来吧，"她说，"我会让你避开风暴"

如今我们之间竖起了一道墙，有些东西已经失去
有太多事我都想当然了，而遭到了误解
想想这一切都始于一个久已忘却的早晨
"进来吧，"她说，"我会让你避开风暴"

哦，警官步履维艰，牧师进退维谷
但这都没什么要紧，唯一算数的只有厄运
那独眼的送葬者吹着一个无用的号角
"进来吧，"她说，"我会让你避开风暴"

我听见新生儿嚎啕像鸽子的哀鸣
坏牙的老人们陷于无爱的苦境
我理解你的问题了吗，老兄，是不是孤独而无望？
"进来吧，"她说，"我会让你避开风暴"

在山顶的一个小村子里，他们为我的衣服赌博
我指望得到救助，他们却给了我致命的剂量
我付出了我的天真，得到的只是嘲笑
"进来吧，"她说，"我会让你避开风暴"

哦，我生活在异国但我一定会跨越边界
美行走于刀锋，我总有一天会得到它
我多想把时钟调回上帝和她都刚刚诞生的那一刻
"进来吧，"她说，"我会让你避开风暴"

Shelter from the Storm

'Twas in another lifetime, one of toil and blood
When blackness was a virtue and the road was full of mud
I came in from the wilderness, a creature void of form
"Come in," she said, "I'll give you shelter from the storm"

And if I pass this way again, you can rest assured
I'll always do my best for her, on that I give my word
In a world of steel-eyed death, and men who are fighting to
    be warm
"Come in," she said, "I'll give you shelter from the storm"

Not a word was spoke between us, there was little risk involved
Everything up to that point had been left unresolved
Try imagining a place where it's always safe and warm
"Come in," she said, "I'll give you shelter from the storm"

I was burned out from exhaustion, buried in the hail
Poisoned in the bushes an' blown out on the trail
Hunted like a crocodile, ravaged in the corn
"Come in," she said, "I'll give you shelter from the storm"

Suddenly I turned around and she was standin' there
With silver bracelets on her wrists and flowers in her hair
She walked up to me so gracefully and took my crown of
    thorns
"Come in," she said, "I'll give you shelter from the storm"

Now there's a wall between us, somethin' there's been lost
I took too much for granted, got my signals crossed

Just to think that it all began on a long-forgotten morn
"Come in," she said, "I'll give you shelter from the storm"

Well, the deputy walks on hard nails and the preacher rides
a mount
But nothing really matters much, it's doom alone that
counts
And the one-eyed undertaker, he blows a futile horn
"Come in," she said, "I'll give you shelter from the storm"

I've heard newborn babies wailin' like a mournin' dove
And old men with broken teeth stranded without love
Do I understand your question, man, is it hopeless and
forlorn?
"Come in," she said, "I'll give you shelter from the storm"

In a little hilltop village, they gambled for my clothes
I bargained for salvation an' they gave me a lethal dose
I offered up my innocence and got repaid with scorn
"Come in," she said, "I'll give you shelter from the storm"

Well, I'm livin' in a foreign country but I'm bound to cross
the line
Beauty walks a razor's edge, someday I'll make it mine
If I could only turn back the clock to when God and her
were born
"Come in," she said, "I'll give you shelter from the storm"

大雨倾盆

大雨倾盆

泪水倾盆

这雨水和泪水绵绵无尽

在我的手中月光盈盈

我得到了所有的爱，亲爱的

你多么慷慨

我温和

而又结实如橡树

我眼看着美人烟一样消逝

朋友们会来，朋友们也会走

如果你需要我，亲爱的

我就在这里

我喜欢你的微笑

你指尖的轻触

喜欢你双唇翕动的样子

喜欢你看我时的从容

与你有关的一切如今都让我

难过

红色的小马车

红色的小单车

我不是没有胡闹过，但我知道我喜欢什么

我喜欢你笃定而悠悠爱我的方式

当我走时，亲爱的

我要带你一起走

人生很悲哀

人生是一场失败

你所能做的就是做你必须做的

你做你必须做的，把它做好

我会为你这样做，亲爱的

你是否明白？

Buckets of Rain

Buckets of rain
Buckets of tears
Got all them buckets comin' out of my ears
Buckets of moonbeams in my hand
I got all the love, honey baby
You can stand

I been meek
And hard like an oak
I seen pretty people disappear like smoke
Friends will arrive, friends will disappear
If you want me, honey baby
I'll be here

Like your smile
And your fingertips
Like the way that you move your lips
I like the cool way you look at me
Everything about you is bringing me
Misery

Little red wagon
Little red bike
I ain't no monkey but I know what I like
I like the way you love me strong and slow
I'm takin' you with me, honey baby
When I go

Life is sad

Life is a bust
All ya can do is do what you must
You do what you must do and ya do it well
I'll do it for you, honey baby
Can't you tell?

取决于我

所有事情都变得越来越糟，金钱什么也改变不了
死亡始终尾随着我们，但至少我听到你蓝知更鸟的歌声
现在得有人亮出底牌了，时间是个敌人
我知道你已一去不返，我想那一定责任在我

如果我曾想到过就绝不会那么做，我想我会听之任之
如果我像别人以为的那样生活，我的内心应早已死去
我只是太倔强了，从不愿被强迫性的疯狂控制
有的人必须心怀高远，我想这要取决于我

哦，"联合中央"[1]正在退出，兰花正在开放
我只留下了一件干净的 T 恤，闻着有种陈旧的芳香
十四个月里我只笑过一次，而且并不自觉
得有人寻找你的踪迹，我想那一定责任在我

那真让我意想不到，当你用你的做法背叛了我
我差点说服自己相信没发生什么大的变化
铁面的老牧师偷偷塞给我万能钥匙

---

1. "联合中央"，美国人寿保险公司，成立于 1867 年，2013 年被兼并。

得有人开启你的心扉，他说这要取决于我

哦，我看着你一点点远去，消失在军官俱乐部
我应该跟着你进去，然而我没有入场券
于是我守了一宿到天亮，希望我们中的一个能获得自由
而当曙光漫过桥上，我知道这要取决于我

哦，我当邮局职员时唯一做过的好事
是把你的照片从我工作间旁的墙上扯下来
尽力保护你的身份，我是不是个傻瓜？
你看着有些疲惫，我的朋友，我想这也许责任在我

哦，我和某人见过面，还不得不摘下我的帽子
她是我需要和喜爱的一切，但我不会为此动摇
生活可以何等甜蜜，那可怕的事实吓到了我
但她并没有将我打动，我想那必须取决于我

我们都听过登山宝训[1]，我知道它极其复杂
可比起碎玻璃反射出来的东西，它的价值并没有更多
当你拿到的多过你需要的，你就会受到惩罚
得有人讲讲这个故事，我想那一定责任在我

---

1. 登山宝训，指耶稣基督在山上传道所说的话，见《新约·马太福音》5-7。

唉，杜普雷今晚来雷鸟咖啡馆拉皮条

克里斯特尔想跟他说话，我只好装作往别处看

唉，没有你我就不得安宁，亲爱的，我需要你的陪伴

但是你不打算迈出这一步，我想那一定责任在我

瓶子里有张便条，你可以把它交给埃丝特尔

你对她颇有些怀疑，但其实真没什么值得一说

我们都听到过一些传言，现在都已经成为历史

得有人掉些眼泪，我想那必须取决于我

走吧，小伙子们，动动你们的手，人生是一出哑剧

县里的头头们说你们已没有太多时间

那跟在我身后的姑娘，并非我的财产

我们中的一个必须要上路，我想那一定责任在我

假如我们再也不会相遇，宝贝，请记住我

我孤独的吉他是如何为你甜蜜地弹奏那旧日的旋律

口琴挂在我脖子上，我曾为你吹奏，免费的

再没有别人能吹出那种调子，你知道那都取决于我

Up to Me

Everything went from bad to worse, money never changed a
    thing
Death kept followin', trackin' us down, at least I heard your
    bluebird sing
Now somebody's got to show their hand, time is an enemy
I know you're long gone, I guess it must be up to me

If I'd thought about it I never would've done it, I guess I
    would've let it slide
If I'd lived my life by what others were thinkin', the heart
    inside me would've died
I was just too stubborn to ever be governed by enforced
    insanity
Someone had to reach for the risin' star, I guess it was up to
    me

Oh, the Union Central is pullin' out and the orchids are in
    bloom
I've only got me one good shirt left and it smells of stale
    perfume
In fourteen months I've only smiled once and I didn't do it
    consciously
Somebody's got to find your trail, I guess it must be up to
    me

It was like a revelation when you betrayed me with your
    touch
I'd just about convinced myself that nothin' had changed
    that much

The old Rounder in the iron mask slipped me the master
   key
Somebody had to unlock your heart, he said it was up to me

Well, I watched you slowly disappear down into the officers'
   club
I would've followed you in the door but I didn't have a
   ticket stub
So I waited all night 'til the break of day, hopin' one of us
   could get free
When the dawn came over the river bridge, I knew it was
   up to me

Oh, the only decent thing I did when I worked as a postal
   clerk
Was to haul your picture down off the wall near the cage
   where I used to work
Was I a fool or not to try to protect your identity?
You looked a little burned out, my friend, I thought it
   might be up to me

Well, I met somebody face to face and I had to remove
   my hat
She's everything I need and love but I can't be swayed by
   that
It frightens me, the awful truth of how sweet life can be
But she ain't a-gonna make me move, I guess it must be up
   to me

We heard the Sermon on the Mount and I knew it was too
   complex
It didn't amount to anything more than what the broken
   glass reflects

When you bite off more than you can chew you pay the penalty
Somebody's got to tell the tale, I guess it must be up to me

Well, Dupree came in pimpin' tonight to the Thunderbird Café
Crystal wanted to talk to him, I had to look the other way
Well, I just can't rest without you, love, I need your company
But you ain't a-gonna cross the line, I guess it must be up to me

There's a note left in the bottle, you can give it to Estelle
She's the one you been wond'rin' about, but there's really nothin' much to tell
We both heard voices for a while, now the rest is history
Somebody's got to cry some tears, I guess it must be up to me

So go on, boys, and play your hands, life is a pantomime
The ringleaders from the county seat say you don't have all that much time
And the girl with me behind the shades, she ain't my property
One of us has got to hit the road, I guess it must be up to me

And if we never meet again, baby, remember me
How my lone guitar played sweet for you that old-time melody
And the harmonica around my neck, I blew it for you, free
No one else could play that tune, you know it was up to me

呼号蓝调

哦，我走了整整一夜
听着教堂的钟声
是的，我走了整整一夜
听着教堂的钟声
这不是有人需要宽恕
就是有些事我也许做错了

哦，你的朋友过来找你
我不知道说些什么
哦，你的朋友过来找你
我不知道说些什么
我没法当面告诉他们
亲爱的你已经离开了

哦，孩子们哭着要妈妈
我告诉他们："妈妈旅行去了"
哦，孩子们哭着要妈妈
我告诉他们："妈妈旅行去了"
哦，我像在针尖上行走
唯恐说漏嘴了

哦，我注视着路过的陌生人
想着也许会看见你
是的，我注视着路过的陌生人
想着也许会看见你
可太阳在天空转动
又一天过去了

Call Letter Blues

Well, I walked all night long
Listenin' to them church bells tone
Yes, I walked all night long
Listenin' to them church bells tone
Either someone needing mercy
Or maybe something I've done wrong

Well, your friends come by for you
I don't know what to say
Well, your friends come by for you
I don't know what to say
I just can't face up to tell 'em
Honey you just went away

Well, children cry for mother
I tell them, "Mother took a trip"
Well, children cry for mother
I tell them, "Mother took a trip"
Well, I walk on pins and needles
I hope my tongue don't slip

Well, I gaze at passing strangers
In case I might see you
Yes, I gaze at passing strangers
In case I might see you
But the sun goes around the heavens
And another day just drives on through

Carolina born and bred
Love to hunt the little quail
Got a hundred-acre spread
Got some huntin dogs for sale
    CHORUS
Reggie Jackson at the plate
Seein' nothin' but the curve
Swing too early or too late
Got to eat what catfish serve.
    CHORUS

Even Billy Virdon grins
When the Fish is in the game
Every season twenty wins
Gonna make the Hall of Fame.

渴望
Desire

厄土 曹疏影 译

《渴望》是鲍勃·迪伦的第十七张专辑，发行于 1976 年 1月，从商业性角度而言，也是他最成功的专辑之一。

这张专辑共收录了十六首歌曲，其中十首的歌词由迪伦和词作家雅克·利维（Jacques Levy）共同创作而成。此外，与小提琴演奏家斯卡利特·里韦拉（Scarlet Rivera）、歌手埃米卢·哈里斯（Emmylou Harris）的合作，在一定程度上也拓宽了迪伦的创作视野，这使得此专辑明显呈现出与前作不一样的音乐风格，但在内容上并没有与以往的作品完全断裂。迪伦回归到针砭时弊的旧路，对当时美国一些光怪陆离的社会现象与人物遭遇进行了大胆而直接的揭露。其中，关注因种族问题而遭受司法不公的黑人拳手的《"飓风"》及描写黑帮人物的《乔伊》，均引起了不小争议。有评论表示，迪伦在这张专辑中所塑造的"被压迫的英雄"这一形象，或许是他当下内心感受的直观反映。另外，创作此专辑时，迪伦刚与第一任妻子萨拉离婚，其中不少歌曲弥漫着苦楚失落之感。

　　本专辑中的《"飓风"》《乔伊》及附加歌词由本人翻译，其余数首由曹疏影女士翻译。

厄土

"飓风" [1]
（与雅克·利维合作）

枪击声响彻酒吧的夜晚

帕蒂·瓦伦丁自楼上下来

她看到了血泊中的酒保

哭喊道："天，他们全遇害了！"

"飓风"的故事开始了

这个被当局定罪的男人

因为他从没干过的事

要不是入狱，他本可成为

世界冠军

帕蒂看到有三具尸体倒在那里

一个叫贝洛的男人诡异地走来走去

"不是我干的，"他说着举起了双手

"我只是在抢劫收银柜，希望你能明白

---

1. 即鲁宾·卡特（Rubin Carter，1937—2014），美国黑人中量级拳王，因拳风富于侵略性和力量感，而获"飓风"的绰号。1966年，他被判谋杀三人而入狱，但从未认罪。1985年，他在不断的上诉中被改判无罪而获释。在卡特服刑期间，迪伦阅读了他的自传，前往探望，并与雅克·利维一同创作了这首歌。

我看到了他们的离开，"他停了下来

"我们中最好有人叫警察来"

于是帕蒂就报了警

随后警察来到现场，红色警灯闪烁不停

在新泽西这个闷热的夜晚

与此同时，远在小镇另一端

鲁宾·卡特正和一群朋友开车兜风

当一位警察把他拽到了路边

这位中量级拳王的头号争夺者

并不知会遇到怎样的倒霉事情

就和上次和上上次一样

在佩特森事情就是如此

如果你是黑人最好别出现在大街上

除非你想引火上身

艾尔弗雷德·贝洛有个同伙，他向警察供述

他和亚瑟·德克斯特·布拉德利当时正在外面逡巡

他说："我看到两个男人跑了出来，体型中等

跳进了一辆外州牌照的白色轿车"

帕蒂·瓦伦丁小姐点了点头

警察说："等一下，伙计们，这个人还没死"

他们随后把他送去了医院

虽然这个人近乎失明

但他们告诉他，他可以指认罪犯

清晨四点，他们拖来了鲁宾

把他带到医院，弄上了楼

那个受伤的男人睁开一只快瞎的眼，抬头看着他

说："你们干吗带他来这儿？不是他！"

是的，这是"飓风"的故事

这个被当局定罪的男人

因为他从没干过的事

要不是入狱，他本可成为

世界冠军

四个月以后，贫民区沸腾了

鲁宾正在南美为名誉而战

亚瑟·德克斯特·布拉德利仍深陷抢劫案里

警察不断向他施压，就为了找人担罪

"记得酒吧里发生的那场谋杀案吗？"

"记得你说你看到过逃逸的车辆吗？"

"你觉得你愿意和法律合作？"

"想想看，那晚你看到的逃犯会不会是那个拳击手？"

"别忘了你是白人"

亚瑟·德克斯特·布拉德利说："我真的不确定"

警察说："像你这样的可怜家伙该缓口气了

我们给你找了份汽车旅馆的工作，也正和你朋友贝洛谈

既然你们现在不想再回监狱，那就做个好小伙

你们会为社会作出贡献

那个狗娘养的很嚣张，越来越嚣张

我们要把他送到牢里去

我们要把这一案三命算到他头上

他别指望能当'绅士吉姆'[1]"

鲁宾只用一记重拳就能送对手出局

但他从不怎么喜欢谈论这事

他会说，这是我的工作，干活赚钱而已

一旦结束，我就会立刻上路

去个极美的地方

那儿鳟鱼溪潺潺，空气清新

还可以沿着小径骑马

但他们却把他关进了监狱

在那里他们试图把人变成鼠

---

1. 即美国前重量级拳王詹姆斯·约翰·科贝特（James J. Corbett，1866—1933），他被称作"现代拳击之父"，因为人正直，被人们称为"绅士吉姆"。

鲁宾所有的牌都被事先做了标记[1]

审讯就是场"猪马戏"[2]，他没有任何生机

法官把鲁宾的证人当作来自贫民窟的酒鬼

不管是视他为闹革命的流浪汉的白人

还是把他看成发疯的黑鬼的黑人

没人怀疑他曾扣动了扳机

尽管他们无法出示那把枪

但公诉人说他就是凶手

纯白人的陪审团表示同意

鲁宾·卡特遭遇了不实的审判

罪名是一级谋杀，猜猜谁作的证？

贝洛和布拉德利，他们都撒下了弥天大谎

就连报纸也赶来凑热闹

这样的一个人的一生

怎能任由傻瓜玩弄于股掌？

看着他明显遭到陷害

我不禁为生活在把公正当儿戏的土地上

而感到羞耻

---

1. 给牌做标记，是赌桌上常见的老千方式，这里意指鲁宾被恶意构陷。

2. "猪马戏"，为迪伦原创词，指代那些通过捏造事实和证据来达成预期结果的法庭闹剧或虚假审判。

现在，所有罪人都穿着外套打着领带

自在地喝着马提尼看着日出

而鲁宾却像佛陀样盘坐在十英尺见方的囚室里

一名无辜者被困在活生生的地狱里

这就是"飓风"的故事

这个故事不会终结，除非他们洗刷了他的罪名

把他服刑的时光都还回来

要不是入狱，他本可成为

世界冠军

Hurricane

(with Jacques Levy)

Pistol shots ring out in the barroom night
Enter Patty Valentine from the upper hall
She sees the bartender in a pool of blood
Cries out, "My God, they killed them all!"
Here comes the story of the Hurricane
The man the authorities came to blame
For somethin' that he never done
Put in a prison cell, but one time he could-a been
The champion of the world

Three bodies lyin' there does Patty see
And another man named Bello, movin' around mysteriously
"I didn't do it," he says, and he throws up his hands
"I was only robbin' the register, I hope you understand
I saw them leavin'," he says, and he stops
"One of us had better call up the cops"
And so Patty calls the cops
And they arrive on the scene with their red lights flashin'
In the hot New Jersey night

Meanwhile, far away in another part of town
Rubin Carter and a couple of friends are drivin' around
Number one contender for the middleweight crown
Had no idea what kinda shit was about to go down
When a cop pulled him over to the side of the road
Just like the time before and the time before that
In Paterson that's just the way things go

If you're black you might as well not show up on the street
'Less you wanna draw the heat

Alfred Bello had a partner and he had a rap for the cops
Him and Arthur Dexter Bradley were just out prowlin'
    around
He said, "I saw two men runnin' out, they looked like
    middleweights
They jumped into a white car with out-of-state plates"
And Miss Patty Valentine just nodded her head
Cop said, "Wait a minute, boys, this one's not dead"
So they took him to the infirmary
And though this man could hardly see
They told him that he could identify the guilty men

Four in the mornin' and they haul Rubin in
Take him to the hospital and they bring him upstairs
The wounded man looks up through his one dyin' eye
Says, "Wha'd you bring him in here for? He ain't the guy!"
Yes, here's the story of the Hurricane
The man the authorities came to blame
For somethin' that he never done
Put in a prison cell, but one time he could-a been
The champion of the world

Four months later, the ghettos are in flame
Rubin's in South America, fightin' for his name
While Arthur Dexter Bradley's still in the robbery game
And the cops are puttin' the screws to him, lookin' for
    somebody to blame
"Remember that murder that happened in a bar?"
"Remember you said you saw the getaway car?"
"You think you'd like to play ball with the law?"

"Think it might-a been that fighter that you saw runnin'
    that night?"
"Don't forget that you are white"

Arthur Dexter Bradley said, "I'm really not sure"
Cops said, "A poor boy like you could use a break
We got you for the motel job and we're talkin' to your
    friend Bello
Now you don't wanta have to go back to jail, be a nice fellow
You'll be doin' society a favor
That sonofabitch is brave and gettin' braver
We want to put his ass in stir
We want to pin this triple murder on him
He ain't no Gentleman Jim"

Rubin could take a man out with just one punch
But he never did like to talk about it all that much
It's my work, he'd say, and I do it for pay
And when it's over I'd just as soon go on my way
Up to some paradise
Where the trout streams flow and the air is nice
And ride a horse along a trail
But then they took him to the jailhouse
Where they try to turn a man into a mouse

All of Rubin's cards were marked in advance
The trial was a pig-circus, he never had a chance
The judge made Rubin's witnesses drunkards from the slums
To the white folks who watched he was a revolutionary bum
And to the black folks he was just a crazy nigger
No one doubted that he pulled the trigger
And though they could not produce the gun
The D.A. said he was the one who did the deed

And the all-white jury agreed

Rubin Carter was falsely tried
The crime was murder "one," guess who testified?
Bello and Bradley and they both baldly lied
And the newspapers, they all went along for the ride
How can the life of such a man
Be in the palm of some fool's hand?
To see him obviously framed
Couldn't help but make me feel ashamed to live in a land
Where justice is a game

Now all the criminals in their coats and their ties
Are free to drink martinis and watch the sun rise
While Rubin sits like Buddha in a ten-foot cell
An innocent man in a living hell
That's the story of the Hurricane
But it won't be over till they clear his name
And give him back the time he's done
Put in a prison cell, but one time he could-a been
The champion of the world

伊西丝

（与雅克·利维合作）

五月第五天，我和伊西丝结婚
但我没法和她长久相处
所以我剃光头发，策马绝尘
去那未知野乡，我不会误入歧途的地方

我来到一处高地，黑暗与光明同在
阴阳界一线，切穿小镇中间
我在右手边的柱子上拴好小马
走进一家洗衣房去把我衣服洗了

角落里一个男人凑过来向我借火
我即刻知道他并非泛泛之辈
他说："你在找什么容易得手的吗？"
我说："我没钱。"他说："这没关系"

那夜我们就启程，奔向北方严寒
我给了他毯子，他就告诉我一些情况
我问："咱们去哪？"他说我们四天后就回来了

我说："我听过的消息这个最好了！"

我想着绿松石，想着黄金
我想着钻石，和世上最大的项链
当我们骑马穿过峡谷，穿过酷寒
我想着伊西丝，她是怎么看待我这么的鲁莽

她怎样告诉我，有一天我们将会重逢
还有下次结婚时，一切都将不同
如果我能够再等等，先做她的朋友
她说过的那么多美事，我不能一一记起

来到金字塔脚下，塔群嵌在冰中
他说："这里有我要找的木乃伊
把它搬出来，我就能卖个好价钱了"
这时我才知道，他肚子里打的什么主意

风鬼嚎，雪肆虐
我们凿了一整夜，我们凿到大清早
凿到他死了，厄运可别传给我
但我下定决心，必须继续下去

终于闯进墓穴，但棺材空空如也

没有珠宝，我以为会有的都没有
我这才看出我的拍档不过是在客套
我肯定是疯了，才采纳他的提议

我拽起他的尸体，拖进坟墓
把他扔进棺材里，把盖盖回去
我匆匆祈祷了一下，然后心满意足
打马回程去找伊西丝，只为告诉她我爱她

她就站在牧场上，过去小溪奔涌的地方
我困得睁不开眼，亟需倒在一张床上
而我从东边出现，眼里满是阳光
那次我骂了她，然后策马向前

她说："你去哪了？"我说："没去哪"
她说："你变了。"我说："哦，没吧"
她说："你就那么消失了。"我说："很自然啊"
她说："你留下来吗？"我说："嗯，会吧"

伊西丝，哦伊西丝，你这神秘的孩子
把我拉向你身边的，也是令我陷入疯狂的
我还记得你笑起来的样子
在五月第五天的细雨中

Isis
(with Jacques Levy)

I married Isis on the fifth day of May
But I could not hold on to her very long
So I cut off my hair and I rode straight away
For the wild unknown country where I could not go wrong

I came to a high place of darkness and light
The dividing line ran through the center of town
I hitched up my pony to a post on the right
Went in to a laundry to wash my clothes down

A man in the corner approached me for a match
I knew right away he was not ordinary
He said, "Are you lookin' for somethin' easy to catch?"
I said, "I got no money." He said, "That ain't necessary"

We set out that night for the cold in the North
I gave him my blanket, he gave me his word
I said, "Where are we goin'?" He said we'd be back by the
    fourth
I said, "That's the best news that I've ever heard"

I was thinkin' about turquoise, I was thinkin' about gold
I was thinkin' about diamonds and the world's biggest
    necklace
As we rode through the canyons, through the devilish cold
I was thinkin' about Isis, how she thought I was so reckless

How she told me that one day we would meet up again
And things would be different the next time we wed
If I only could hang on and just be her friend
I still can't remember all the best things she said

We came to the pyramids all embedded in ice
He said, "There's a body I'm tryin' to find
If I carry it out it'll bring a good price"
'Twas then that I knew what he had on his mind

The wind it was howlin' and the snow was outrageous
We chopped through the night and we chopped through
    the dawn
When he died I was hopin' that it wasn't contagious
But I made up my mind that I had to go on

I broke into the tomb, but the casket was empty
There was no jewels, no nothin', I felt I'd been had
When I saw that my partner was just bein' friendly
When I took up his offer I must-a been mad

I picked up his body and I dragged him inside
Threw him down in the hole and I put back the cover
I said a quick prayer and I felt satisfied
Then I rode back to find Isis just to tell her I love her

She was there in the meadow where the creek used to rise
Blinded by sleep and in need of a bed
I came in from the East with the sun in my eyes
I cursed her one time then I rode on ahead

She said, "Where ya been?" I said, "No place special"
She said, "You look different." I said, "Well, not quite"

She said, "You been gone." I said, "That's only natural"
She said, "You gonna stay?" I said, "Yeah, I jes might"

Isis, oh, Isis, you mystical child
What drives me to you is what drives me insane
I still can remember the way that you smiled
On the fifth day of May in the drizzlin' rain

莫桑比克

（与雅克·利维合作）

我喜欢待在莫桑比克
明媚的天空如水湛蓝
爱人们全都跳着贴面舞
最好待上一两个星期

莫桑比克有许多美女
日子很长足够你浪漫
人人都爱停下来聊聊
给你所寻找的特别的人一次机会
又或者只是一瞥说声你好

躺在她旁边，身畔是碧海
伸伸臂就摸到她的手
低声诉说你的秘密心情
魔幻地带魔力弥漫

是离开莫桑比克的时候了
要跟沙和海说再见了

你转身看那最后一眼

你知道了为何这里独一无二

在莫桑比克的明媚海滩

那些可爱的人儿自由自在

Mozambique
(with Jacques Levy)

I like to spend some time in Mozambique
The sunny sky is aqua blue
And all the couples dancing cheek to cheek
It's very nice to stay a week or two

There's lot of pretty girls in Mozambique
And plenty time for good romance
And everybody likes to stop and speak
To give the special one you seek a chance
Or maybe say hello with just a glance

Lying next to her by the ocean
Reaching out and touching her hand
Whispering your secret emotion
Magic in a magical land

And when it's time for leaving Mozambique
To say goodbye to sand and sea
You turn around to take a final peek
And you see why it's so unique to be
Among the lovely people living free
Upon the beach of sunny Mozambique

再来一杯咖啡
（下面的溪谷）

你气息香甜

双眼似苍穹里两枚宝石

你玉立亭亭，发丝柔滑

散在正枕着的枕头上

但我感受不到浓情

既无感激也没有爱意

你所专情的并非我

而是上空繁星

再来一杯咖啡就上路

再来一杯咖啡我就走

去往下面的溪谷

你老爸是个亡命徒

以流浪为业

他会教你怎样选对路

怎样扔飞刀

他看管自己的王国

所以并无陌生人闯入
他嗓音颤抖地
想再唤来一碟食物

再来一杯咖啡就上路
再来一杯咖啡我就走
去往下面的溪谷

你妹妹能洞悉未来
就像你母亲和你
你一直不会读书写字
架子上也没什么书
你的愉悦却无止境
你的声音像草地鹨
但你的心如汪洋
神秘而幽暗

再来一杯咖啡就上路
再来一杯咖啡我就走
去往下面的溪谷

One More Cup of Coffee
(Valley Below)

Your breath is sweet
Your eyes are like two jewels in the sky
Your back is straight, your hair is smooth
On the pillow where you lie
But I don't sense affection
No gratitude or love
Your loyalty is not to me
But to the stars above

One more cup of coffee for the road
One more cup of coffee 'fore I go
To the valley below

Your daddy he's an outlaw
And a wanderer by trade
He'll teach you how to pick and choose
And how to throw the blade
He oversees his kingdom
So no stranger does intrude
His voice it trembles as he calls out
For another plate of food

One more cup of coffee for the road
One more cup of coffee 'fore I go
To the valley below

Your sister sees the future

Like your mama and yourself
You've never learned to read or write
There's no books upon your shelf
And your pleasure knows no limits
Your voice is like a meadowlark
But your heart is like an ocean
Mysterious and dark

One more cup of coffee for the road
One more cup of coffee 'fore I go
To the valley below

哦，姐妹

（与雅克·利维合作）

哦，姐妹，当我躺进你怀抱
别把我当作陌生人
我们的父不喜欢你这样做
你要明白那样的危险

哦，姐妹，难道我不是你的兄弟？
难道我不值得你关爱？
难道我们在尘世不是一样为了
去爱，去追随他的指引？

我们一起长大
从摇篮到坟墓
死去又重生
再被神秘地救赎

哦，姐妹，当我敲响你的门
别转过身去，那样会制造忧伤
时间如海洋，但终结于岸
明天兴许你就见不到我

Oh, Sister
(with Jacques Levy)

Oh, sister, when I come to lie in your arms
You should not treat me like a stranger
Our Father would not like the way that you act
And you must realize the danger

Oh, sister, am I not a brother to you
And one deserving of affection?
And is our purpose not the same on this earth
To love and follow His direction?

We grew up together
From the cradle to the grave
We died and were reborn
And then mysteriously saved

Oh, sister, when I come to knock on your door
Don't turn away, you'll create sorrow
Time is an ocean but it ends at the shore
You may not see me tomorrow

乔伊 [1]

（与雅克·利维合作）

生于布鲁克林的雷德胡克，谁知道是哪一年

他睁开双眼聆听手风琴曲

总是待在外面随便什么地方

人们问他为什么非得那样，他回答说："哦，不为什么"

拉里是长子，乔伊排行倒数第二

人们叫乔伊"疯子"，叫老幺"爆炸小孩"

有人说他们靠赌博和跑码 [2] 为生

似乎他们经常纠缠在黑帮和警察之间

乔伊，乔伊

街头的王，泥土之子

乔伊，乔伊

究竟是什么使得他们要来除掉你？

---

1. 乔伊·加洛（Joey Gallo，1929—1972），纽约黑手党"科伦坡家族"头目之一，绰号"疯子乔伊""金毛乔伊"。1972 年死于谋杀。

2. 跑码，指在美国的非法数字博彩生意中，从赌徒或码民那里收取赌注、投注号码及派发奖金。

有种说法称他们杀掉了自己的对手，但事实远非如此

没人确切地知道他们当时真正在哪里

当他们试图勒死拉里，乔伊简直暴跳如雷

那夜他出去寻仇，以为自己刀枪不入

那场战斗在破晓时分爆发，清空了整个街区

乔伊和他的兄弟们遭受了可怕的失败

直到他们冒险冲出防线，俘获了五名俘虏

他们把俘虏藏到了地下室，称他们为"生手"

人质们瑟瑟发抖，当他们听到有人大声叫喊

"让我们把这地方炸上天，让爱迪生联合电气公司去
    顶罪"

但是乔伊走上前，他抬起手，说："我们可不是那种人

我们要的是安宁平静，好回去继续干活"

乔伊，乔伊

街头的王，泥土之子

乔伊，乔伊

究竟是什么使得他们要来除掉你？

警方追捕他，称他为史密斯先生

他们以同谋罪逮捕了他，但他们从不确定是和谁

"几点了？"法官见到乔伊时这么问他

"差五分十点，"乔伊答道。法官说："这就是你最终所得"[1]

他在阿提卡服了十年刑，阅读尼采和威廉·赖希[2]

有次他们判他单独监禁，以制止他教唆煽动其他囚犯

他最亲近的朋友都是黑人，因为他们似乎明白

手戴镣铐在这社会中是什么滋味

1971 年被释放时，他已消瘦了些许

但他的穿着打扮像是吉米·卡格尼[3]，我发誓他看上去

　棒极了

他试着想办法回到被他抛下的生活里

他对老板说："我回来了，现在我得要回属于我的东西"

乔伊，乔伊

街头的王，泥土之子

乔伊，乔伊

---

1. 此处双关，法官问乔伊时间，乔伊回答"差五分十点"，法官称以此为乔伊的量刑，即五到十年。

2. 威廉·赖希（Wilhelm Reich, 1897—1957），美籍奥地利裔心理学家、社会学家，被视作美国 20 世纪四五十年代性解放运动的精神领袖之一。

3. 即詹姆斯·卡格尼（James Cagney, 1899—1986），美国演员，以扮演强盗、表现罪犯的病态心理而驰名。

究竟是什么使得他们要来除掉你？

是真的，他在最后的岁月里不愿意带枪
"我身边有太多孩子，"他说，"他们应该永远不知道
　这回事"
然而，他却径直走进了他终身死敌的俱乐部
抢空了收银柜，说：“告诉他们，是疯子乔伊干的”

后来有一天，他们在纽约的一家蛤蜊餐厅[1]干掉了他
他拿起餐叉时就看到这事找上了门
他掀翻了桌子保护家人
而后跌撞着冲到了小意大利的街上

乔伊，乔伊
街头的王，泥土之子
乔伊，乔伊
究竟是什么使得他们要来除掉你？

姊妹杰奎琳和卡梅拉以及母亲玛丽都在哭泣
我听他最好的朋友弗兰基说：“他没有死，他只是睡着了”

---

1. 即翁贝托蛤蜊餐厅（Umberto's Clam House），当时位于曼哈顿小意大利桑树街 132 号。

我看到老人掉转豪车车头朝向坟墓

我猜他是要最后说一次再见，向这个他没能搭救回来的
　孩子

总统街[1]的太阳变得寒冷，布鲁克林的居民陷入了哀伤

人们说在他出生的那所房子附近的老教堂里有一场弥撒

如果有一天上主自天堂俯察他护佑的世界

我知道那些射杀他的人将会领受应得的报应

乔伊，乔伊

街头的王，泥土之子

乔伊，乔伊

究竟是什么使得他们要来除掉你？

---

1. 总统街，位于纽约布鲁克林的一条街道，乔伊所属的黑手党"科伦坡家族"
总部就在这条街上。

Joey
(with Jacques Levy)

Born in Red Hook, Brooklyn, in the year of who knows
    when
Opened up his eyes to the tune of an accordion
Always on the outside of whatever side there was
When they asked him why it had to be that way, "Well," he
    answered, "just because"

Larry was the oldest, Joey was next to last
They called Joe "Crazy," the baby they called "Kid Blast"
Some say they lived off gambling and runnin' numbers too
It always seemed they got caught between the mob and the
    men in blue

Joey, Joey
King of the streets, child of clay
Joey, Joey
What made them want to come and blow you away?

There was talk they killed their rivals, but the truth was far
    from that
No one ever knew for sure where they were really at
When they tried to strangle Larry, Joey almost hit the roof
He went out that night to seek revenge, thinkin' he was
    bulletproof

The war broke out at the break of dawn, it emptied out the
    streets

Joey and his brothers suffered terrible defeats
Till they ventured out behind the lines and took five
   prisoners
They stashed them away in a basement, called them
   amateurs

The hostages were tremblin' when they heard a man exclaim
"Let's blow this place to kingdom come, let Con Edison
   take the blame"
But Joey stepped up, he raised his hand, said, "We're not
   those kind of men
It's peace and quiet that we need to go back to work again"

Joey, Joey
King of the streets, child of clay
Joey, Joey
What made them want to come and blow you away?

The police department hounded him, they called him Mr.
   Smith
They got him on conspiracy, they were never sure who with
"What time is it?" said the judge to Joey when they met
"Five to ten," said Joey. The judge says, "That's exactly what
   you get"

He did ten years in Attica, reading Nietzsche and Wilhelm
   Reich
They threw him in the hole one time for tryin' to stop
   a strike
His closest friends were black men 'cause they seemed to
   understand
What it's like to be in society with a shackle on your hand

When they let him out in '71 he'd lost a little weight
But he dressed like Jimmy Cagney and I swear he did look great
He tried to find the way back into the life he left behind
To the boss he said, "I have returned and now I want what's mine"

Joey, Joey
King of the streets, child of clay
Joey, Joey
Why did they have to come and blow you away?

It was true that in his later years he would not carry a gun
"I'm around too many children," he'd say, "they should never know of one"
Yet he walked right into the clubhouse of his lifelong deadly foe
Emptied out the register, said, "Tell 'em it was Crazy Joe"

One day they blew him down in a clam bar in New York
He could see it comin' through the door as he lifted up his fork
He pushed the table over to protect his family
Then he staggered out into the streets of Little Italy

Joey, Joey
King of the streets, child of clay
Joey, Joey
What made them want to come and blow you away?

Sister Jacqueline and Carmela and mother Mary all did weep
I heard his best friend Frankie say, "He ain't dead, he's just asleep"

Then I saw the old man's limousine head back towards the
grave
I guess he had to say one last goodbye to the son that he
could not save

The sun turned cold over President Street and the town of
Brooklyn mourned
They said a mass in the old church near the house where he
was born
And someday if God's in heaven overlookin' His preserve
I know the men that shot him down will get what they
deserve

Joey, Joey
King of the streets, child of clay
Joey, Joey
What made them want to come and blow you away?

杜兰戈罗曼史

（与雅克·利维合作）

红辣椒在炙热的阳光里
尘与土在我的脸和斗篷上
我和玛格达莱娜大逃亡
自觉这次我们能成功

我的吉他卖给了面包师的儿子
换来了些面包屑和一个藏身之处
但我还能弄来另外一把琴
好在逃亡时弹给玛格达莱娜听

亲爱的，不要哭
上帝眷顾我们
马儿很快就把我们带到杜兰戈
抓住我，我的命根子[1]
沙漠就快走过
很快你就可以跳起方丹戈舞

---

1. 此节第一、二、四行歌词原文为西班牙语，以下相同句子皆同。

路过阿兹特克人的废墟，吾民的鬼魂

石上马蹄得得好像响板

夜里我梦见村里尖塔上的铃钟

看见拉蒙那流血的面庞

饭馆里把他撂倒的是我吗？

握着枪的是我的手吗？

来吧，让我们一起飞，我的玛格达莱娜

狗在吠，干了就是干了

亲爱的，不要哭

上帝眷顾我们

马儿很快就把我们带到杜兰戈

抓住我，我的命根子

沙漠就快走过

很快你就可以跳起方丹戈舞

我们会坐在斗牛场的荫凉里

看年轻的斗牛士独立场中

我们会喝着龙舌兰酒，待在祖父们待过的地方

当他们和维拉将军一起骑马进入托雷翁

然后神父会诵念起古老祷文

在小镇这一端的小教堂里
我会穿着新靴戴上一只金耳环
你会身着婚纱钻石闪耀

道路很长但结局近了
狂欢节已经开始
上帝之面将显现
他那黑曜石的双眼如蛇一般

亲爱的，不要哭
上帝眷顾我们
马儿很快就把我们带到杜兰戈
抓住我，我的命根子
沙漠就快走过
很快你就可以跳起方丹戈舞

我听到的是一声响雷吗？
我的头在震动，一道疼痛锋利
坐到我身边来，什么也别说
哦，难道是我被杀了吗？

快，玛格达莱娜，拿起我的枪
看天上雷电闪耀过群山

瞄准一点我的小爱人

我们可能过不了今晚

亲爱的，不要哭

上帝眷顾我们

马儿很快就把我们带到杜兰戈

抓住我，我的命根子

沙漠就快走过

很快你就可以跳起方丹戈舞

Romance in Durango

(with Jacques Levy)

Hot chili peppers in the blistering sun
Dust on my face and my cape
Me and Magdalena on the run
I think this time we shall escape

Sold my guitar to the baker's son
For a few crumbs and a place to hide
But I can get another one
And I'll play for Magdalena as we ride

No llores, mi querida
Dios nos vigila
Soon the horse will take us to Durango
Agarrame, mi vida
Soon the desert will be gone
Soon you will be dancing the fandango

Past the Aztec ruins and the ghosts of our people
Hoofbeats like castanets on stone
At night I dream of bells in the village steeple
Then I see the bloody face of Ramon

Was it me that shot him down in the cantina
Was it my hand that held the gun?
Come, let us fly, my Magdalena
The dogs are barking and what's done is done

No llores, mi querida
Dios nos vigila
Soon the horse will take us to Durango
Agárrame, mi vida
Soon the desert will be gone
Soon you will be dancing the fandango

At the corrida we'll sit in the shade
And watch the young torero stand alone
We'll drink tequila where our grandfathers stayed
When they rode with Villa into Torreón

Then the padre will recite the prayers of old
In the little church this side of town
I will wear new boots and an earring of gold
You'll shine with diamonds in your wedding gown

The way is long but the end is near
Already the fiesta has begun
The face of God will appear
With His serpent eyes of obsidian

No llores, mi querida
Dio nos vigila
Soon the horse will take us to Durango
Agárrame, mi vida
Soon the desert will be gone
Soon you will be dancing the fandango

Was that the thunder that I heard?
My head is vibrating, I feel a sharp pain
Come sit by me, don't say a word
Oh, can it be that I am slain?

Quick, Magdalena, take my gun
Look up in the hills, that flash of light
Aim well my little one
We may not make it through the night

No llores, mi querida
Dios nos vigila
Soon the horse will take us to Durango
Agarrame, mi vida
Soon the desert will be gone
Soon you will be dancing the fandango

黑钻石湾

（与雅克·利维合作）

白色走廊上

她打着领带，戴着巴拿马帽

护照上贴着另一张脸

来自另一时空

她和那张脸一点都不像

这段日子的余烬

在狂风中零落

她走过大理石地板

赌场里有人叫她进去

她笑了，走另一条路

此时最后的船启航，月亮隐退

从黑钻石湾

晨光破晓，希腊人下楼

他要一段绳子，还要笔来写字

"抱歉，先生，"[1] 接待员说

---

1. 原文为法语。

小心摘下土耳其毡帽

"我没听错吧？"

而黄雾升起之际

希腊人飞快上了二楼

她在螺旋楼梯上与他擦肩而过

以为他是那个苏联大使

她正搭腔，而他走开了

此时风起云涌，棕榈枝四散

在黑钻石湾

士兵坐在风扇下

正和卖他戒指的矮子做交易

电光闪烁，电灯熄灭

接待员惊醒，开始大叫

"你们能看见东西吗？"

希腊人出现在二楼

光着脚，绳子绕在脖子上

赌场里，输家点亮蜡烛

说："再开一副牌吧"

但庄家说："请等等"[1]

此时雨落如注，鹤群飞去

---

1. 原文为法语。

从黑钻石湾

接待员听到女人在笑

当时他正环视四周情况，士兵强硬起来

想去抓女人的手

他说："我这有枚戒指，值不少银子"

而她说："这还不够"

说完她跑上楼收好行李

一辆马车等在路边

她经过希腊人的房间，门锁着

门上贴了张字条，手写着"请勿打扰"

但她不管，还是敲响了门

此时太阳正在下山，音乐响起

在黑钻石湾

"我说几句就走！"

但希腊人说："走开。"他把椅子踢翻在地

把自己吊在水晶灯上

她哭叫："帮帮忙，大事不好了

请快开门！"

就在这时火山爆发

熔岩自高高的山口流涌而下

士兵和矮子蜷缩在角落里

想着那禁忌之恋

接待员却说：“这事每天都发生”

此时群星下沉，原野灼伤

在黑钻石湾

岛屿缓慢下沉

赌场里，输家终于把庄家赢光

庄家说：“太迟了

你可以拿回你的钱，但我不知道

在坟墓里你怎么花掉”

矮子咬士兵的耳朵

地板坍塌了，地下室的锅炉炸开

而她来到外面的阳台上，一个陌生人告诉她

“亲爱的，我非常爱你[1]”

她流泪然后开始祈祷

此时烈焰正猛，烟雾漫开

从黑钻石湾

一个晚上我独自坐在洛杉矶的家里

看着七点钟新闻里的老克朗凯特[2]

---

1. 原文为法语。
2. 即沃尔特·克朗凯特（Walter Cronkite，1916—2009），美国著名记者，1962年至1981年间任哥伦比亚广播公司《晚间新闻》主播，被誉为“美国最受信任的人”。

说是发生了地震

除了一顶巴拿马帽子

一双旧了的希腊鞋，什么都没剩下

似乎没事发生过

于是我关了电视，又去拿了一罐啤酒

就像每次你这样转身

就听到又一个倒霉的故事

也真的没人能说些什么

而我不管怎样，也从没计划过要

去黑钻石湾

Black Diamond Bay
(with Jacques Levy)

Up on the white veranda
She wears a necktie and a Panama hat
Her passport shows a face
From another time and place
She looks nothin' like that
And all the remnants of her recent past
Are scattered in the wild wind
She walks across the marble floor
Where a voice from the gambling room is callin' her to
    come on in
She smiles, walks the other way
As the last ship sails and the moon fades away
From Black Diamond Bay

As the mornin' light breaks open, the Greek comes down
And he asks for a rope and a pen that will write
"Pardon, monsieur," the desk clerk says
Carefully removes his fez
"Am I hearin' you right?"
And as the yellow fog is liftin'
The Greek is quickly headin' for the second floor
She passes him on the spiral staircase
Thinkin' he's the Soviet Ambassador
She starts to speak, but he walks away
As the storm clouds rise and the palm branches sway
On Black Diamond Bay

A soldier sits beneath the fan
Doin' business with a tiny man who sells him a ring
Lightning strikes, the lights blow out
The desk clerk wakes and begins to shout
"Can you see anything?"
Then the Greek appears on the second floor
In his bare feet with a rope around his neck
While a loser in the gambling room lights up a candle
Says, "Open up another deck"
But the dealer says, "Attendez-vous, s'il vous plaît"
As the rain beats down and the cranes fly away
From Black Diamond Bay

The desk clerk heard the woman laugh
As he looked around the aftermath and the soldier got tough
He tried to grab the woman's hand
Said, "Here's a ring, it cost a grand"
She said, "That ain't enough"
Then she ran upstairs to pack her bags
While a horse-drawn taxi waited at the curb
She passed the door that the Greek had locked
Where a handwritten sign read, "Do Not Disturb"
She knocked upon it anyway
As the sun went down and the music did play
On Black Diamond Bay

"I've got to talk to someone quick!"
But the Greek said, "Go away," and he kicked the chair to
    the floor
He hung there from the chandelier
She cried, "Help, there's danger near
Please open up the door!"
Then the volcano erupted

And the lava flowed down from the mountain high above
The soldier and the tiny man were crouched in the corner
Thinking of forbidden love
But the desk clerk said, "It happens every day"
As the stars fell down and the fields burned away
On Black Diamond Bay

As the island slowly sank
The loser finally broke the bank in the gambling room
The dealer said, "It's too late now
You can take your money, but I don't know how
You'll spend it in the tomb"
The tiny man bit the soldier's ear
As the floor caved in and the boiler in the basement blew
While she's out on the balcony, where a stranger tells her
"My darling, je vous aime beaucoup"
She sheds a tear and then begins to pray
As the fire burns on and the smoke drifts away
From Black Diamond Bay

I was sittin' home alone one night in L.A.
Watchin' old Cronkite on the seven o'clock news
It seems there was an earthquake that
Left nothin' but a Panama hat
And a pair of old Greek shoes
Didn't seem like much was happenin'
So I turned it off and went to grab another beer
Seems like every time you turn around
There's another hard-luck story that you're gonna hear
And there's really nothin' anyone can say
And I never did plan to go anyway
To Black Diamond Bay

萨拉

我躺在沙丘上,我看着天
孩子们还小,在海滩上玩
你来到我背后,我看着你绕过
你总是那么近,伸手可及

萨拉,萨拉
是什么让你变心?
萨拉,萨拉
你就在眼前,却难以描画

我还能看到他们拎着小桶玩沙
奔向海水小桶就灌满
我还能看到贝壳从他们的小手中掉落
小鬼们一个跟着一个退回沙丘

萨拉,萨拉
可爱的圣洁天使,我一生的挚爱
萨拉,萨拉
闪耀的宝石,神秘的妻

入夜后躺在林间篝火旁

在葡萄牙酒吧喝白朗姆酒

孩子们玩跳跳蛙听听《白雪公主》

而你还在滨海萨凡纳的集市游逛

萨拉，萨拉

这些如在眼前，我永不忘记

萨拉，萨拉

爱你我永不会后悔

我还能听见卫理公会的钟响

我接受了治疗，才熬了过来

在切尔西旅馆几日不睡

为了给你写首《满眼忧伤的低地女士》[1]

萨拉，萨拉

无论去到哪里，我们都不分离

萨拉啊，萨拉

美丽的女士，我心的最爱

我是怎么遇见你的？我也不知道

———————

1. 迪伦将这首歌收录在 1966 年的专辑《金发叠金发》中。

信使把我送进了热带风暴

你在那里时，适值冬天，月光映雪

而在莲池巷时，天气暖和

萨拉啊，萨拉

穿印花裙的天蝎座斯芬克斯

萨拉，萨拉

你一定要原谅我的不中用

现在沙滩荒芜只剩一些海藻

一艘老船停在岸旁

我需要你时你总会回应

你给予我一张地图，一把你家门的钥匙

萨拉啊，萨拉

魅惑的宁芙手持弓箭

萨拉啊，萨拉

千万别离开我，千万别走

Sara

I laid on a dune, I looked at the sky
When the children were babies and played on the beach
You came up behind me, I saw you go by
You were always so close and still within reach

Sara, Sara
Whatever made you want to change your mind?
Sara, Sara
So easy to look at, so hard to define

I can still see them playin' with their pails in the sand
They run to the water their buckets to fill
I can still see the shells fallin' out of their hands
As they follow each other back up the hill

Sara, Sara
Sweet virgin angel, sweet love of my life
Sara, Sara
Radiant jewel, mystical wife

Sleepin' in the woods by a fire in the night
Drinkin' white rum in a Portugal bar
Them playin' leapfrog and hearin' about Snow White
You in the marketplace in Savanna-la-Mar

Sara, Sara
It's all so clear, I could never forget
Sara, Sara
Lovin' you is the one thing I'll never regret

I can still hear the sounds of those Methodist bells
I'd taken the cure and had just gotten through
Stayin' up for days in the Chelsea Hotel
Writin' "Sad-Eyed Lady of the Lowlands" for you

Sara, Sara
Wherever we travel we're never apart
Sara, oh Sara
Beautiful lady, so dear to my heart

How did I meet you? I don't know
A messenger sent me in a tropical storm
You were there in the winter, moonlight on the snow
And on Lily Pond Lane when the weather was warm

Sara, oh Sara
Scorpio Sphinx in a calico dress
Sara, Sara
You must forgive me my unworthiness

Now the beach is deserted except for some kelp
And a piece of an old ship that lies on the shore
You always responded when I needed your help
You gimme a map and a key to your door

Sara, oh Sara
Glamorous nymph with an arrow and bow
Sara, oh Sara
Don't ever leave me, don't ever go

被弃的爱

我能听到钥匙的转动
我被内心的小丑欺骗
我以为他正直，但他却是自负的
哦，有些事告诉我，我身负枷锁

我的主保圣人正在和鬼魂交战
我最需要他时，总是寻他不见
西班牙的月亮在山上升起
我的心告诉我，我还爱着你

我自燃烧的月亮回到了这座小镇
我在大街上看到了你，开始痴迷
我爱看你在镜前穿衣
在我最终离开前，你就不能让我进你房间一回？

每个人都乔装打扮
来掩饰他们双眼背后所抛却的东西
而我，我无法掩盖自己的本性
我会跟随孩子们，无论他们去哪里

我加入自由的游行队伍

但只要我还爱你，自由便无从谈起

我还须忍受多久这样的虐待

在我放手前，你就不能让我看你微笑一回？

这场游戏我已认输，我要离开了

黄金罐[1]纯属虚构

那宝藏不可能被寻觅的人们寻得

他们的诸神已死，他们的女王在教堂里

我们坐在空无一人的剧院里，相吻

我请求你把我从你的名单上删去

我的理智告诉我是时候做出改变

我的心告诉我我爱你，但你如此陌生

又一次在午夜，在墙边

卸下你的浓妆，脱去你的披巾

你就不能从王座上、从你端坐的地方走下来？

让我在放弃之前再感受一回你的爱意

---

1. 黄金罐，爱尔兰民间传说，小矮妖（leprechaun）在彩虹尽头藏着装满黄金和财宝的坛罐。

Abandoned Love

I can hear the turning of the key
I've been deceived by the clown inside of me
I thought that he was righteous but he's vain
Oh, something's a-telling me I wear the ball and chain

My patron saint is a-fighting with a ghost
He's always off somewhere when I need him most
The Spanish moon is rising on the hill
But my heart is a-tellin' me I love ya still

I come back to the town from the flaming moon
I see you in the streets, I begin to swoon
I love to see you dress before the mirror
Won't you let me in your room one time 'fore I finally
   disappear?

Everybody's wearing a disguise
To hide what they've got left behind their eyes
But me, I can't cover what I am
Wherever the children go I'll follow them

I march in the parade of liberty
But as long as I love you I'm not free
How long must I suffer such abuse
Won't you let me see you smile one time before I turn you
   loose?

I've given up the game, I've got to leave
The pot of gold is only make-believe

The treasure can't be found by men who search
Whose gods are dead and whose queens are in the church

We sat in an empty theater and we kissed
I asked ya please to cross me off-a your list
My head tells me it's time to make a change
But my heart is telling me I love ya but you're strange

One more time at midnight, near the wall
Take off your heavy makeup and your shawl
Won't you descend from the throne, from where you sit?
Let me feel your love one more time before I abandon it

"鲶鱼" [1]
（与雅克·利维合作）

懒洋洋的体育场之夜
"鲶鱼"在投手丘
"三振出局。"裁判说
击球手必须退场坐下

"鲶鱼"，百万富翁
没人能像"鲶鱼"样投球

曾在芬利先生的农场工作
但那老男人从不发薪
所以他戴上手套拿起装备
在某一天逃离

"鲶鱼"，百万富翁
没人能像"鲶鱼"样投球

---

1. 即詹姆斯·亨特（James A. Hunter，1946—1999），绰号"鲶鱼"，美国棒球运动员，司职投手，1976 年在纽约洋基队，于 1987 年入选美国国家棒球名人堂。

去到洋基队[1]所在的地方

穿上细条纹的西装

抽着定制的雪茄

穿着鳄鱼皮的靴子

"鲶鱼", 百万富翁

没人能像"鲶鱼"样投球

在卡罗莱纳出生和长大

喜欢猎杀小鹌鹑

拥有上百英亩的农场

拥有许多待售的猎犬

"鲶鱼", 百万富翁

没人能像"鲶鱼"样投球

雷吉·杰克逊[2]在本垒

1. 即纽约洋基队, 美国职业棒球大联盟中隶属美国联盟东区的棒球队, 成立于 1901 年, 主场位于纽约布朗克斯区。
2. 即雷金纳德·杰克逊 (Reginald Martinez Jackson, 1946—), 美国棒球运动员, 司职击球手, 1976 年在巴尔的摩金莺队, 于 1993 年入选美国国家棒球名人堂。

正目不斜视盯着曲线球

挥棒太早或太迟

都会吃一记"鲶鱼"的开球

"鲶鱼",百万富翁

没人能像"鲶鱼"样投球

只要"鲶鱼"在赛场上

比利·马丁[1]就会咧嘴笑

每季二十场胜利

即将进入名人堂

"鲶鱼",百万富翁

没人能像"鲶鱼"样投球

---

1. 比利·马丁(Billy Martin,1928—1989),洋基队经理,曾带领球队赢得两次世界冠军。

Catfish
(with Jacques Levy)

Lazy stadium night
Catfish on the mound
"Strike three," the umpire said
Batter have to go back and sit down

Catfish, million-dollar-man
Nobody can throw the ball like Catfish can

Used to work on Mr. Finley's farm
But the old man wouldn't pay
So he packed his glove and took his arm
An' one day he just ran away

Catfish, million-dollar-man
Nobody can throw the ball like Catfish can

Come up where the Yankees are
Dress up in a pinstripe suit
Smoke a custom-made cigar
Wear an alligator boot

Catfish, million-dollar-man
Nobody can throw the ball like Catfish can

Carolina born and bred
Love to hunt the little quail
Got a hundred-acre spread

Got some huntin' dogs for sale

Catfish, million-dollar-man
Nobody can throw the ball like Catfish can

Reggie Jackson at the plate
Seein' nothin' but the curve
Swing too early or too late
Got to eat what Catfish serve

Catfish, million-dollar-man
Nobody can throw the ball like Catfish can

Even Billy Martin grins
When the Fish is in the game
Every season twenty wins
Gonna make the Hall of Fame

Catfish, million-dollar-man
Nobody can throw the ball like Catfish can

金纺车

烟雾弥漫的秋夜，群星高悬于天

我看到一叶帆船横渡海湾消失不见

桉树悬立在大街上

而后我转过头，因你在走近我

月光洒在水面，渔夫的女儿，漂浮进我的房间

带来了一辆金纺车

我们先在永恒的圣所旁濯足

而后我们的影子相逢，而后我们饮酒

我看到饥饿的云飘升在你脸上

而后泪珠滚落，何其苦涩

而后你飘走了，在一个夏日，在野花盛放的地方

带走了你的金纺车

我在惨淡的光里走过大桥

在夜晚的大门间，所有的车辆都被拆除了

我看到颤抖的狮子生有莲花样的尾巴

而后我掀起你的面纱，吻你的双唇

但你离开了，而后我能忆起的唯有芬芳的气息

和你的金纺车

Golden Loom

Smoky autumn night, stars up in the sky
I see the sailin' boats across the bay go by
Eucalyptus trees hang above the street
And then I turn my head, for you're approachin' me
Moonlight on the water, fisherman's daughter, floatin' in to
    my room
With a golden loom

First we wash our feet near the immortal shrine
And then our shadows meet and then we drink the wine
I see the hungry clouds up above your face
And then the tears roll down, what a bitter taste
And then you drift away on a summer's day where the
    wildflowers bloom
With your golden loom

I walk across the bridge in the dismal light
Where all the cars are stripped between the gates of night
I see the trembling lion with the lotus flower tail
And then I kiss your lips as I lift your veil
But you're gone and then all I seem to recall is the smell of
    perfume
And your golden loom

丽塔·梅 [1]

（与雅克·利维合作）

丽塔·梅，丽塔·梅

你让你的身体挡着道

你竟如此该死的冷漠

但你的思想正是我要的

你让我气喘吁吁

在你身边我感到一无所有

丽塔·梅

丽塔·梅，丽塔·梅

你怎么会产生那种想法？

你什么时候看到过光？

难道你没有害怕过？

你让我燃烧，我正在转变

但我知道我必须学习

丽塔·梅

---

1. 丽塔·梅，常被认为指丽塔·梅·布朗（Rita Mae Brown，1944— ），
美国作家、和平主义者和女性主义者。

所有的朋友都告诉我
如果我厮混在你身边
我就会变得盲目
但我知道在你抱住我时
你的脑海里真的
一定在想着什么

丽塔·梅，丽塔·梅
躺在一堆干草上
你是否记得你去过哪里？
你置身在怎样疯狂的地方？
我不得不起身前往大学
因为你就是一本知识之书
丽塔·梅

Rita May

(with Jacques Levy)

Rita May, Rita May
You got your body in the way
You're so damn nonchalant
But it's your mind that I want
You got me huffin' and a-puffin'
Next to you I feel like nothin'
Rita May

Rita May, Rita May
How'd you ever get that way?
When do you ever see the light?
Don't you ever feel a fright?
You got me burnin' and I'm turnin'
But I know I must be learnin'
Rita May

All my friends have told me
If I hang around with you
That I'll go blind
But I know that when you hold me
That there really must be somethin'
On your mind

Rita May, Rita May
Laying in a stack of hay
Do you remember where you been?
What's that crazy place you're in?

I'm gonna have to go to college
'Cause you are the book of knowledge
Rita May

七天

七天，还有七天她就会来临
我将在车站等着她到达
还有七天，我需要做的就是活着

她离开时我尚是孩童
自从我见过了她的微笑，就无法忘记她的双眼
她的脸庞比天上的太阳还闪耀

我还好，在等待时我还好
或许犹豫不决的过错，只要再坚持
七天，都将会消失

在山谷中亲吻
在小径里行窃
在每寸路途中争斗
尝试变得温柔
对我记忆中某个总比白天还明亮的夜晚的
某个人

七天，还有连续七天

就像我期盼的，她即将到来
我自北方而来的美丽战友

在山谷中亲吻
在小径里行窃
在每寸路途中争斗
尝试变得温柔
对我记忆中某个总比白天还明亮的夜晚的
某个人

Seven Days

Seven days, seven more days she'll be comin'
I'll be waiting at the station for her to arrive
Seven more days, all I gotta do is survive

She been gone ever since I been a child
Ever since I seen her smile, I ain't forgotten her eyes
She had a face that could outshine the sun in the skies

I been good, I been good while I been waitin'
Maybe guilty of hesitatin', I just been holdin' on
Seven more days, all that'll be gone

There's kissing in the valley
Thieving in the alley
Fighting every inch of the way
Trying to be tender
With somebody I remember
In a night that's always brighter'n the day

Seven days, seven more days that are connected
Just like I expected, she'll be comin' on forth
My beautiful comrade from the north

There's kissing in the valley
Thieving in the alley
Fighting every inch of the way
Trying to be tender
With somebody I remember
In a night that's always brighter'n the day

手语

你用手语
对我说话
当时我正在小咖啡馆里
吃一块三明治
还差一刻三点钟
但我无法回应
你的手语
你利用了这一点
这让我沮丧
你就不能发出任何声音吗？

就在那间面包房附近
被欺诈包围
告诉她我的故事
虽然我仍在那里
她是否明白我仍在乎？

林克·雷[1]正在

---

1. 林克·雷（Link Wray，1929—2005），美国摇滚吉他手，强力和弦的发明者，影响了几代重金属和朋克的吉他演奏者。

我投钱的点唱机里演奏

因我说过的那些话

如此被误解

他对我没什么好处

你用手语

对我说话

当时我正在小咖啡馆里

吃一块三明治

还差一刻三点钟

但我无法回应

你的手语

你利用了这一点

这让我沮丧

你就不能发出任何声音吗？

Sign Language

You speak to me
In sign language
As I'm eating a sandwich
In a small café
At a quarter to three
But I can't respond
To your sign language
You're taking advantage
Bringing me down
Can't you make any sound?

'Twas there by the bakery
Surrounded by fakery
Tell her my story
Still I'm still there
Does she know I still care?

Link Wray was playin'
On a jukebox I was payin'
For the words I was sayin'
So misunderstood
He didn't do me no good

You speak to me
In sign language
As I'm eating a sandwich
In a small café
At a quarter to three
But I can't respond

To your sign language
You're taking advantage
Bringing me down
Can't you make any sound?

金钱蓝调
（与雅克·利维合作）

坐在这儿，思索着
钱都去哪儿了？
坐在这儿，思索着
钱都去哪儿了？
唉，我把钱给了我的女人
她可不能再拿到钱了

昨夜出门
买了两个鸡蛋一片火腿
昨夜出门
买了两个鸡蛋一片火腿
账单共计三美元十美分
而我甚至都没买果酱

有人找我
索要租金
有人找我
索要租金

唉，我拉开抽屉寻

但所有的钱都花光了

唉，唉

没有任何银行户头

唉，唉

没有任何银行户头

想去开设一个

但我也没有足够的钱

一切都已膨胀[1]

就像汽车轮胎

一切都已膨胀

就像汽车轮胎

唉，那人来收回了我那辆雪佛兰

我很庆幸我藏起了自己的旧吉他

来我身边吧，妈妈[2]

赶快缓解我当下的金钱危机吧

来我身边吧，妈妈

---

1. 膨胀，与"通货膨胀"双关。
2. 妈妈，口语中又有"情人""妻子"之意。

赶快缓解我当下的金钱危机吧

我需要得到一些支持

也只有你明白该怎么做

Money Blues
(with Jacques Levy)

Sittin' here thinkin'
Where does the money go
Sittin' here thinkin'
Where does the money go
Well, I give it to my woman
She ain't got it no more

Went out last night
Bought two eggs and a slice of ham
Went out last night
Bought two eggs and a slice of ham
Bill came to three dollars and ten cents
And I didn't even get no jam

Man came around
Askin' for the rent
Man came around
Askin' for the rent
Well, I looked into the drawer
But the money's all been spent

Well, well
Ain't got no bank account
Well, well
Ain't got no bank account
Went down to start one
But I didn't have the right amount

Everything's inflated
Like a tire on a car
Everything's inflated
Like a tire on a car
Well, the man came and took my Chevy back
I'm glad I hid my old guitar

Come to me, mama
Ease my money crisis now
Come to me, mama
Ease my money crisis now
I need something to support me
And only you know how

Midwives stroll between jupiter & apollo   *I stared into the eyes - Ages roll - up on jupiter & apollo*   *Destiny's faces*
Struggling babes past (Between the sheets of...
A messenger arrives with a blck nightengale   *— (with) her favor*   *on the steps*
~~there~~ I see her on the square &   I cannot help but follow
Follow her down to the fountain   where she's lifting her veil
                                                her (old) rags & her (tail)

          baby be still
~~Here I am~~ she said, can y spare me a moment's passion
Can I shine yr shoes, print yr money or mark yr cards
What frozen truths ~~can~~ yr brave ~~me~~ souls imagine
Does yr hearts have the courage for the changing of the guards

街道合法
Street Legal

奚密　译

《街道合法》是鲍勃·迪伦的第十八张专辑，1978 年 6 月 15 日由哥伦比亚唱片公司发行。1977 年，迪伦跟结合了十一年的妻子萨拉离婚，并争取到子女抚养权。他回到家乡明尼苏达州，开始筹划下一轮的世界巡回演唱会。1978 年 2 月他回到美国，4 月在南加州的圣莫妮卡市录制了这张新专辑。

不同于此前的专辑，他在伴奏乐队里加入了萨克斯风和伴唱歌手，有意将表达模式做得时髦些，类似拉斯维加斯的音乐秀风格。有人说他在模仿"猫王"埃尔维斯·普雷斯利（Elvis Presley）（他甚至聘用了曾为"猫王"伴奏的乐手），也有人说他模仿歌手和作曲家尼尔·戴蒙德（Neil Diamond）。专辑上的新歌仍具备迪伦的深度和神秘，但是它们似乎和大乐队的配乐格格不入。也因此，发行后这张专辑得到的评价褒贬不一，在美国的销路远远不如前面两张——1975 年的《轨道上的血》和 1976 年的《渴望》，所幸在欧洲仍然成绩斐然。直到今天，歌迷对《街道合法》的感受仍相当两极。

《街道合法》也预示了迪伦的信仰转向：生为犹太人，他在1979 年受洗为基督徒。在接下来的两年里，他连续出了两张基督教主题的唱片。虽然他后来又皈依了正统犹太教，基督教仍然对他的作品具有明显的影响。

奚密

守卫换岗

十六个年头
十六幅旗帜团结在原野上
善良的牧羊人在哀悼
绝境中的男人和女人们分离
各自在飘飘落叶下展翅

福气在呼唤
从阴影中我迈着步伐，走向市场
商人和小偷渴望权力，我最后一场交易失败
她芬芳一如她诞生的草原
在盛夏的傍晚，高塔之旁

冷血的月亮
队长在庆典的高处等待
将他的思念寄给心爱的女郎
她深褐色的脸庞高深莫测
队长很沮丧但仍相信他的爱会有回报

他们剃去她的秀发
她彷徨在朱庇特和阿波罗之间

信差来到带着一只黑色的夜莺

我在楼梯间看见她而不可自抑地跟着她

跟着她走过喷水池在那里他们揭开她的面纱

我脚步踉跄

我骑马跨过那些沟渠里的毁灭

针线还在一个心形的文身下面缝补

叛逃的神父和不忠的年青女巫们

把我送给你的花随手送走

镜子的宫殿

映照出那些犬兵 [1]

没有尽头的路和嚎哭的钟声

空房间里她的回忆得到保护

天使们的声音向旧时代的灵魂耳语

她将他唤醒

四十八小时之后，太阳露了脸

在打破的链索、山月桂和滚石旁

---

1. 犬兵，美国印第安夏延族部落的战士组织，夏延人迷信狗会转生为勇士，故名。以上两行歌词指涉罗伯特·斯通的小说《镜厅》(A Hall of Mirrors) 和《亡命之徒》(Dog Soldiers)。

她恳求知道他将采取什么措施
他拖她下来而她紧紧抓住他金色的卷发

绅士们，他说
我不需要你们的组织，我擦亮过你们的鞋
我移过你们的山丘[1]也给过你们提点
但是伊甸园着火了，你们或者准备被消灭
或者你们的心必须有勇气面对守卫换岗

和平将来临
带着火轮上的宁静和灿烂
但我们得不到报酬，当她的假偶像倒下
当残酷的死亡投降，它苍白的鬼魂撤退
在宝剑国王和宝剑皇后之间

1.《新约·马太福音》17:20，耶稣说："你们若有信心像一粒芥菜种，就是对这座山说，'你从这边挪到那边'，它也必挪去……"

Changing of the Guards

Sixteen years
Sixteen banners united over the field
Where the good shepherd grieves
Desperate men, desperate women divided
Spreading their wings 'neath the falling leaves

Fortune calls
I stepped forth from the shadows, to the marketplace
Merchants and thieves, hungry for power, my last deal gone
   down
She's smelling sweet like the meadows where she was born
On midsummer's eve, near the tower

The cold-blooded moon
The captain waits above the celebration
Sending his thoughts to a beloved maid
Whose ebony face is beyond communication
The captain is down but still believing that his love will be
   repaid

They shaved her head
She was torn between Jupiter and Apollo
A messenger arrived with a black nightingale
I seen her on the stairs and I couldn't help but follow
Follow her down past the fountain where they lifted her veil

I stumbled to my feet
I rode past destruction in the ditches
With the stitches still mending 'neath a heart-shaped tattoo

Renegade priests and treacherous young witches
Were handing out the flowers that I'd given to you

The palace of mirrors
Where dog soldiers are reflected
The endless road and the wailing of chimes
The empty rooms where her memory is protected
Where the angels' voices whisper to the souls of previous
    times

She wakes him up
Forty-eight hours later, the sun is breaking
Near broken chains, mountain laurel and rolling rocks
She's begging to know what measures he now will be taking
He's pulling her down and she's clutching on to his long
    golden locks

Gentlemen, he said
I don't need your organization, I've shined your shoes
I've moved your mountains and marked your cards
But Eden is burning, either brace yourself for elimination
Or else your hearts must have the courage for the changing
    of the guards

Peace will come
With tranquillity and splendor on the wheels of fire
But will bring us no reward when her false idols fall
And cruel death surrenders with its pale ghost retreating
Between the King and the Queen of Swords

新的小马

我曾经有一匹小马，它的名字是路西法
我有一匹小马，它的名字是路西法
它摔断了腿，它需要一枪
我发誓我的痛超过它可能受到的痛

有时候我猜想 X 小姐到底在想什么
有时候我猜想 X 小姐到底在想什么
你知道她的个性那么甜美
我从不知道这可怜的姑娘将对我做些什么

我有一匹新的小马，它会狐步、大步慢跑和侧对步
是的，我有一匹新的小马，它会狐步、大步慢跑和侧对步
它的后腿非常健壮
头上的鬃毛又长又黑

是啊，一大清早我看见门口你的投影
一大清早我看见门口你的投影
现在我没必要问任何人
我知道你来为了何事

他们说你在使巫毒教巫术，你的双脚自动行走

他们说你在使巫毒教巫术，我看见你双脚自动行走

哦，宝贝，你一直祈祷的那个神

会把你许愿给别人的回报到你身上

过来小马，我，我想再一次爬到你身上

过来小马，我，我想再一次爬到你身上

是啊，你那么使坏难对付

但是我爱你，是的我爱你

New Pony

Once I had a pony, her name was Lucifer
I had a pony, her name was Lucifer
She broke her leg and she needed shooting
I swear it hurt me more than it could ever have hurted her

Sometimes I wonder what's going on in the mind of Miss X
Sometimes I wonder what's going on in the mind of Miss X
You know she got such a sweet disposition
I never know what the poor girl's gonna do to me next

I got a new pony, she knows how to fox-trot, lope and pace
Well, I got a new pony, she knows how to fox-trot, lope and
    pace
She got great big hind legs
And long black shaggy hair above her face

Well now, it was early in the mornin', I seen your shadow
    in the door
It was early in the mornin', I seen your shadow in the door
Now, I don't have to ask nobody
I know what you come here for

They say you're usin' voodoo, your feet walk by themselves
They say you're usin' voodoo, I seen your feet walk by
    themselves
Oh, baby, that god you been prayin' to
Is gonna give ya back what you're wishin' on someone else

Come over here pony, I, I wanna climb up one time on you

Come over here pony, I, I wanna climb up one time on you
Well, you're so bad and nasty
But I love you, yes I do

宝贝，停止哭泣

宝贝，你曾经和坏人一起落到谷底
但是你已回到你归属的所在
宝贝，把我的手枪给我拿来
蜜糖，我已分辨不出对和错

宝贝，请停止哭泣，停止哭泣，停止哭泣
宝贝，请停止哭泣，停止哭泣，停止哭泣
宝贝，请停止哭泣
你知道，我知道，太阳永远会照耀
所以宝贝，请停止哭泣因为我的心要碎了

到那河畔去，宝贝
蜜糖，我会在那儿见你
到那河畔去，宝贝
蜜糖，你的车费我付

宝贝，请停止哭泣，停止哭泣，停止哭泣
宝贝，请停止哭泣，停止哭泣，停止哭泣
宝贝，请停止哭泣
你知道，我知道，太阳永远会照耀

所以宝贝，请停止哭泣因为我的心要碎了

如果你寻找援手，宝贝
或者你只是想有人陪伴你
或者只想有个能倾诉的朋友
蜜糖，到我家来看看我

宝贝，请停止哭泣，停止哭泣，停止哭泣
宝贝，请停止哭泣，停止哭泣，停止哭泣
宝贝，请停止哭泣
你知道，我知道，太阳永远会照耀
所以宝贝，请停止哭泣因为我的心要碎了

太多次你受到伤害
我明白你在想什么
是的，我不需要是医生，宝贝
才看得出你爱得疯狂

宝贝，请停止哭泣，停止哭泣，停止哭泣
宝贝，请停止哭泣，停止哭泣，停止哭泣
宝贝，请停止哭泣
你知道，我知道，太阳永远会照耀
所以宝贝，请停止哭泣因为我的心要碎了

Baby, Stop Crying

You been down to the bottom with a bad man, babe
But you're back where you belong
Go get me my pistol, babe
Honey, I can't tell right from wrong

Baby, please stop crying, stop crying, stop crying
Baby, please stop crying, stop crying, stop crying
Baby, please stop crying
You know, I know, the sun will always shine
So baby, please stop crying 'cause it's tearing up my mind

Go down to the river, babe
Honey, I will meet you there
Go down to the river, babe
Honey, I will pay your fare

Baby, please stop crying, stop crying, stop crying
Baby, please stop crying, stop crying, stop crying
Baby, please stop crying
You know, I know, the sun will always shine
So baby, please stop crying 'cause it's tearing up my mind

If you're looking for assistance, babe
Or if you just want some company
Or if you just want a friend you can talk to
Honey, come and see about me

Baby, please stop crying, stop crying, stop crying
Baby, please stop crying, stop crying, stop crying

Baby, please stop crying
You know, I know, the sun will always shine
So baby, please stop crying 'cause it's tearing up my mind

You been hurt so many times
And I know what you're thinking of
Well, I don't have to be no doctor, babe
To see that you're madly in love

Baby, please stop crying, stop crying, stop crying
Baby, please stop crying, stop crying, stop crying
Baby, please stop crying
You know, I know, the sun will always shine
So baby, please stop crying 'cause it's tearing up my mind

你的爱是徒劳?

你爱我吗，还是你只是在广发善心？

你需要我的程度有你说的一半吗，抑或你只是心生

　愧疚？

我被伤害过，我心中有谱

所以你不会听见我埋怨

我能够依靠你吗

还是你的爱是徒劳？

难道你跑得太快看不见我需要孤独吗？

当我在黑暗中，你为何来打扰？

你懂我的世界，懂我的族类

还是需要我解释？

你能让我做自己吗

还是你的爱是徒劳？

是的，我上过高山也曾立在风中

我得到也失去过幸福

我曾和国王共餐，曾有人要给我翅膀

我都不认为这些有何稀奇

好吧，我就冒个险，我就去爱上你

如果我是傻瓜，你可以拥有我的日和夜

你会做饭缝衣，你会养花吗

你懂我的痛苦吗？

你愿意赌上一切吗

还是你的爱是徒劳？

Is Your Love in Vain?

Do you love me, or are you just extending goodwill?
Do you need me half as bad as you say, or are you just
    feeling guilt?
I've been burned before and I know the score
So you won't hear me complain
Will I be able to count on you
Or is your love in vain?

Are you so fast that you cannot see that I must have solitude?
When I am in the darkness, why do you intrude?
Do you know my world, do you know my kind
Or must I explain?
Will you let me be myself
Or is your love in vain?

Well I've been to the mountain and I've been in the wind
I've been in and out of happiness
I have dined with kings, I've been offered wings
And I've never been too impressed

All right, I'll take a chance, I will fall in love with you
If I'm a fool you can have the night, you can have the
    morning too
Can you cook and sew, make flowers grow
Do you understand my pain?
Are you willing to risk it all
Or is your love in vain?

先生 [1]
（扬基佬强国传奇）

先生，先生，你知道我们走向何处？

是林肯县路 [2] 还是哈米吉多顿 [3] ？

这条路似乎我曾经走过

这样说有道理吗，先生？

先生，先生，你知道她躲在哪儿吗？

我们骑马将骑多久？

我得用双眼盯着门多久？

会带来任何安慰吗，先生？

恶毒的风仍在上层甲板吹着

一枚铁十字架仍挂在她颈上

军乐队仍在空地上演奏着

在那里她曾拥我入怀说："勿忘我"

---

1. 歌名及歌词中的"先生"原文均为西班牙语。
2. 1878 年当时尚为准州的新墨西哥发生长达五个多月的"林肯县战争"，实质为争夺该县的政治和经济控制权，后被演绎成反抗法律和秩序所代表的腐败和贪婪之战。
3. 哈米吉多顿，末日大决战的战场。见《新约·启示录》16:13-16。

先生，先生，我看得见那漆了颜色的篷车
我闻得到那只龙的尾巴
不能再忍受这份悬疑了
能告诉这里我该联络谁吗，先生？

是的，我脱光下跪前记得的最后一件事
是满满一火车的愚人滞留在磁场里
吉普赛人带着一面破旗和闪亮的戒指
说："小子，这不再是场梦，这是真的"

先生，先生，你知道他们的心跟皮革一样硬
好的，给我一分钟，让我收拾一下心情
我必须让我从地上站起来
当你准备好了我也好了，先生

先生，先生，让我们切断这些电缆
把这些桌子推翻
这地方对我来说已经没有道理可讲
你能告诉我我们在等什么吗，先生？

Señor
(Tales of Yankee Power)

Señor, señor, do you know where we're headin'?
Lincoln County Road or Armageddon?
Seems like I been down this way before
Is there any truth in that, señor?

Señor, señor, do you know where she is hidin'?
How long are we gonna be ridin'?
How long must I keep my eyes glued to the door?
Will there be any comfort there, señor?

There's a wicked wind still blowin' on that upper deck
There's an iron cross still hanging down from around her
    neck
There's a marchin' band still playin' in that vacant lot
Where she held me in her arms one time and said, "Forget
    me not"

Señor, señor, I can see that painted wagon
I can smell the tail of the dragon
Can't stand the suspense anymore
Can you tell me who to contact here, señor?

Well, the last thing I remember before I stripped and
    kneeled
Was that trainload of fools bogged down in a magnetic field
A gypsy with a broken flag and a flashing ring
Said, "Son, this ain't a dream no more, it's the real thing"

Señor, señor, you know their hearts is as hard as leather
Well, give me a minute, let me get it together
I just gotta pick myself up off the floor
I'm ready when you are, señor

Señor, señor, let's disconnect these cables
Overturn these tables
This place don't make sense to me no more
Can you tell me what we're waiting for, señor?

真爱倾向于遗忘

我开始厌倦凝视我宝贝的眼睛
当她在我身边时我难以认出她
我终于明白了没有后悔余地
真爱，真爱，真爱倾向于遗忘

拥抱着我，宝贝靠近我
你告诉我你会诚恳待我
全年每日就像在玩俄罗斯轮盘
真爱，真爱，真爱倾向于遗忘

我躺在芦苇丛中没有任何氧气
我看见你在荒原里置身人群中
看见你飘入永恒然后又回来了
你只需要等待，我告诉你何时

你是催泪者，宝贝，但是我中了你的蛊
你努力工作，宝贝，我对你很了解
但是这地狱中的周末让我汗流浃背
真爱，真爱，真爱倾向于遗忘

我躺在芦苇丛中没有任何氧气
我看见你在荒原里置身人群中
看见你飘入永恒然后又回来了
你只需要等待，我告诉你何时

你属于我，宝贝，这毫无疑问
别抛弃我，宝贝，别出卖我
别让我颠簸从墨西哥到西藏
真爱，真爱，真爱倾向于遗忘

True Love Tends to Forget

I'm getting weary looking in my baby's eyes
When she's near me she's so hard to recognize
I finally realize there's no room for regret
True love, true love, true love tends to forget

Hold me, baby be near
You told me that you'd be sincere
Every day of the year's like playin' Russian roulette
True love, true love, true love tends to forget

I was lyin' down in the reeds without any oxygen
I saw you in the wilderness among the men
Saw you drift into infinity and come back again
All you got to do is wait and I'll tell you when

You're a tearjerker, baby, but I'm under your spell
You're a hard worker, baby, and I know you well
But this weekend in hell is making me sweat
True love, true love, true love tends to forget

I was lyin' down in the reeds without any oxygen
I saw you in the wilderness among the men
Saw you drift into infinity and come back again
All you got to do is wait and I'll tell you when

You belong to me, baby, without any doubt
Don't forsake me, baby, don't sell me out
Don't keep me knockin' about from Mexico to Tibet
True love, true love, true love tends to forget

我们最好商量一下

我觉得我们最好商量一下
也许当我们都清醒的时候
你会理解我只是一个男人
尽了我的全力

这情况只会变得更加艰难
我们又何必无谓地受罪呢？
让我们说结束，各走各的路
在我们腐朽前

你不必害怕深深凝视我的脸庞
我们对彼此做的时间都能抹去

我觉得流离失所，我感到消沉
你表里不一，用的是两面手法
我冒了险，却陷落在走下坡的
一支舞的恍惚里

哦，孩子，你为何要伤害我？
我被流放了，你无法让我改信

我迷失在你精致手段的雾中
双眼蒙上薄翳

你不需要渴望爱情，你不需要孤独一人
宇宙某处总有一个你可以叫作家的地方

我想我大概明天就会离去
即使我得乞求偷窃或借贷
一天半日后路上邂逅很棒
我们望着彼此而笑

但我不觉得这可能发生
就好比一只手鼓掌的掌声
我俩的誓言已破灭被扫到
我们曾共眠的床下

别想我或幻想我们从来不曾拥有的
感谢我们曾共享的一切而且快乐些
我们何必继续透过望远镜看彼此呢？
那样最终我们会吊死在这缠结的麻绳上

哦，宝贝，是新过渡的时候了
我希望我是一位魔术师

我会挥一挥魔杖再重新系上

那我们早已远离的纽带

We Better Talk This Over

I think we better talk this over
Maybe when we both get sober
You'll understand I'm only a man
Doin' the best that I can

This situation can only get rougher
Why should we needlessly suffer?
Let's call it a day, go our own different ways
Before we decay

You don't have to be afraid of looking into my face
We've done nothing to each other time will not erase

I feel displaced, I got a low-down feeling
You been two-faced, you been double-dealing
I took a chance, got caught in the trance
Of a downhill dance

Oh, child, why you wanna hurt me?
I'm exiled, you can't convert me
I'm lost in the haze of your delicate ways
With both eyes glazed

You don't have to yearn for love, you don't have to be alone
Somewheres in this universe there's a place that you can call
    home

I guess I'll be leaving tomorrow
If I have to beg, steal or borrow

It'd be great to cross paths in a day and a half
Look at each other and laugh

But I don't think it's liable to happen
Like the sound of one hand clappin'
The vows that we kept are now broken and swept
'Neath the bed where we slept

Don't think of me and fantasize on what we never had
Be grateful for what we've shared together and be glad
Why should we go on watching each other through a
    telescope?
Eventually we'll hang ourselves on all this tangled rope

Oh, babe, time for a new transition
I wish I was a magician
I would wave a wand and tie back the bond
That we've both gone beyond

今夜你在哪里？
（穿过黑热之旅）

长途火车滚滚驶过大雨

泪滴落在我写的信上

有个女人我渴望触碰我如此想念

但是她漂泊像颗卫星

霓虹灯在绿色烟雾中燃烧

伊丽莎白街上的笑声

石头谷里寂寞的钟声

那儿她曾沐浴在纯热之流中

她爹强调你不能只有街头世故

然而从内心里他做到言行一致

血统纯正的彻罗基人，他向我预测

麻烦将要开始的时间和地点

那充满愤怒的女人怀里有一个婴儿

舞台上是老练的金发脱衣舞娘

她倒拨时钟然后她翻回那一页

没人能写的一本书

哦，今夜你在哪里？

真理很模糊，太深奥也太纯粹

活在其中你只得爆炸

在需要的最后时刻我们完全同意

牺牲是路途上的准则

黎明时我离镇，与马塞尔和圣约翰

坚强的男人被怀疑贬低

我无法告诉她我有的私密想法

但是她总有办法发现

他瞄准正中心但他还是打偏了

她等待着，把花放在架子上

她能感受到我的绝望当我爬上她的秀发

发现了她隐形的自我

道上有猛狮，一个魔鬼逃跑了

一百万个梦消失，一道风景被踩躏

当她的美丽褪色而我看着她解衣

我不会不过也说不定，也可能我会

哦，如果今晚我能找到你

我和我的孪体打架，和我内在的敌人

直到我们两个都倒在路边

胡闹和疾病正一点一点地杀死我

而法律撇过脸不理不睬

你的那群共犯来跟我要零钱

你爱的男人没法保持清白

放错了位置，我的脚在他的脸上

但是他本该待在钱是绿色的地方 [1]

我啃一口禁果的根茎

果汁顺着我的腿流下

然后我对付你的老板，他从不知什么是失去

他从不屈尊求人

这房间黑暗处有一股白钻石的阴沉

和通向星星的一条途径

如果你不信这甜蜜的天堂是有代价的

提醒我给你看我的伤痕

新的一天的黎明时分我终于抵达

---

1. 美元钞票为绿色，而习语中非法收益则以黑色（black money）形容。

如果早晨我在那儿，宝贝，你知道我存活了
我不敢相信，不敢相信我还活着
但是没有了你总觉得不对劲
哦，今夜你在哪里？

Where Are You Tonight?
(Journey Through Dark Heat)

There's a long-distance train rolling through the rain
Tears on the letter I write
There's a woman I long to touch and I miss her so much
But she's drifting like a satellite

There's a neon light ablaze in this green smoky haze
Laughter down on Elizabeth Street
And a lonesome bell tone in that valley of stone
Where she bathed in a stream of pure heat

Her father would emphasize you got to be more than
    streetwise
But he practiced what he preached from the heart
A full-blooded Cherokee, he predicted to me
The time and the place that the trouble would start

There's a babe in the arms of a woman in a rage
And a longtime golden-haired stripper onstage
And she winds back the clock and she turns back the page
Of a book that no one can write
Oh, where are you tonight?

The truth was obscure, too profound and too pure
To live it you have to explode
In that last hour of need, we entirely agreed
Sacrifice was the code of the road

I left town at dawn, with Marcel and St. John
Strong men belittled by doubt
I couldn't tell her what my private thoughts were
But she had some way of finding them out

He took dead-center aim but he missed just the same
She was waiting, putting flowers on the shelf
She could feel my despair as I climbed up her hair
And discovered her invisible self

There's a lion in the road, there's a demon escaped
There's a million dreams gone, there's a landscape being
    raped
As her beauty fades and I watch her undrape
I won't but then again, maybe I might
Oh, if I could just find you tonight

I fought with my twin, that enemy within
'Til both of us fell by the way
Horseplay and disease is killing me by degrees
While the law looks the other way

Your partners in crime hit me up for nickels and dimes
The guy you were lovin' couldn't stay clean
It felt outa place, my foot in his face
But he should-a stayed where his money was green

I bit into the root of forbidden fruit
With the juice running down my leg
Then I dealt with your boss, who'd never known about loss
And who always was too proud to beg

There's a white diamond gloom on the dark side of this
    room
And a pathway that leads up to the stars
If you don't believe there's a price for this sweet paradise
Remind me to show you the scars

There's a new day at dawn and I've finally arrived
If I'm there in the morning, baby, you'll know I've survived
I can't believe it, I can't believe I'm alive
But without you it just doesn't seem right
Oh, where are you tonight?

退伍军人症

有人说是辐射，有人说话筒上有酸性物质
有人说某种结合体让人心变成石头
但不管是什么，它让他们屈膝跪下
哦，退伍军人症

我多希望我能给那年病死的人每人一块钱
揪着领子使他们发烧，让老处女泪水涟涟
现在在我内心深处，它狠狠拧我一下
哦，那退伍军人症

爷爷打独立战争，爸爸打 1812 年战争
叔叔在越南打仗然后又独自打了一场战争
但不管是什么，它来自那些树林
哦，那退伍军人症

Legionnaire's Disease

Some say it was radiation, some say there was acid on the
   microphone
Some say a combination that turned their hearts to stone
But whatever it was, it drove them to their knees
Oh, Legionnaire's disease

I wish I had a dollar for everyone that died within that year
Got 'em hot by the collar, plenty an old maid shed a tear
Now within my heart, it sure put on a squeeze
Oh, that Legionnaire's disease

Granddad fought in a revolutionary war, father in the War
   of 1812
Uncle fought in Vietnam and then he fought a war all by
   himself
But whatever it was, it came out of the trees
Oh, that Legionnaire's disease

Suddenly I turned around, she was standing there
with bracelets on wrists and flowers in her hair
She walked up to me so gracefully and took my crown
of thorns
"Come in" She said "I'll give you shelter from the storm"

慢车开来
Slow Train Coming

胡桑 译

　　《慢车开来》是鲍勃·迪伦第十九张专辑，1979年8月20日由哥伦比亚唱片公司发行。就在这一年，出生于犹太家庭的迪伦宣布自己信仰基督教，作为其将信仰态度正式融入音乐的第一次尝试，整张专辑带有鲜明的宗教色彩。在这些歌曲中，迪伦探寻着在堕落、衰败的现代世界中获得救赎的可能性与艰难，表达了自己对个人信仰和基督教义的思考。在歌词里频繁出现的《圣经》词汇和典故，使他的大部分歌迷感到陌生而无所适从，同时又吸引了许多基督徒听众。

　　专辑在面市后迅速登上美国排行榜第三名，其中《得服务于他人》更成为迪伦接下来三年里最热门的单曲，并为他赢得了格莱美最佳摇滚男歌手奖。歌中所蕴含的宗教主题，在他发行于20世纪80年代的《得救》《来一针爱》专辑中均得到了延续，因而本专辑与这两张专辑一并被称为迪伦的"基督教三部曲"。

胡桑

得服务于他人

你也许是派往英格兰或法兰西的使节
你也许想去赌博，你也许想去跳舞
你也许是世界重量级拳击冠军
你也许是社会名流，戴着一串长长的珍珠项链

但你必须服务于他人，是的没错
你必须服务于他人
嗯，他也许是魔鬼，也许是上帝
但你必须服务于他人

你也许是摇滚歌手，沉迷于在舞台上跳来跳去
你也许有毒品可随意用度，有女人养在笼中
你也许是商人，或者是高明的小偷
他们也许叫你博士，或者他们也许叫你长官

但你必须服务于他人，是的没错
你必须服务于他人
嗯，他也许是魔鬼，也许是上帝
但你必须服务于他人

你也许是州警，你也许是年轻的土耳其人

你也许是某家大型电视台的头儿

你也许富足或穷困，你也许目盲或腿瘸

你也许住在另一个国家，有另一个名字

但你必须服务于他人，是的没错

你必须服务于他人

嗯，他也许是魔鬼，也许是上帝

但你必须服务于他人

你也许是盖住房的建筑工人

你也许住在豪宅里，你也许住在穹顶下

你也许有枪，你也许甚至有坦克

你也许是别人的房东，你也许甚至坐拥数家银行

但你必须服务于他人，是的没错

你必须服务于他人

嗯，他也许是魔鬼，也许是上帝

但你必须服务于他人

你也许是布道者，有着属灵的骄傲

你也许是市议员，暗地里受贿

你也许在理发店工作，你也许懂得如何理发

你也许是他人的情妇，也许是他人的继承人

但你必须服务于他人，是的没错
你必须服务于他人
嗯，他也许是魔鬼，也许是上帝
但你必须服务于他人

也许喜欢穿棉的，也许喜欢穿丝的
也许喜欢喝威士忌，也许喜欢喝牛奶
你也许喜欢吃鱼子酱，你也许喜欢吃面包
你也许睡地板，睡特大号床

但你必须服务于他人，是的没错
你必须服务于他人
嗯，他也许是魔鬼，也许是上帝
但你必须服务于他人

你可以叫我特里，你可以叫我蒂米
你可以叫我鲍比，你可以叫我齐米[1]
你可以叫我 R. J.，你可以叫我雷[2]

---

1. 鲍比，鲍勃的昵称。齐米，迪伦本姓齐默曼的昵称。
2. 源自比尔·萨鲁嘎（Bill Saluga）创造的电视喜剧角色小雷蒙德·J. 约翰逊（Raymond J. Johnson Jr.）的经典台词。

你可以叫我任何名字，但你怎么叫都无所谓

你必须服务于他人，是的没错
你必须服务于他人
嗯，他也许是魔鬼，也许是上帝
但你必须服务于他人

Gotta Serve Somebody

You may be an ambassador to England or France
You may like to gamble, you might like to dance
You may be the heavyweight champion of the world
You may be a socialite with a long string of pearls

But you're gonna have to serve somebody, yes indeed
You're gonna have to serve somebody
Well, it may be the devil or it may be the Lord
But you're gonna have to serve somebody

You might be a rock 'n' roll addict prancing on the stage
You might have drugs at your command, women in a cage
You may be a businessman or some high-degree thief
They may call you Doctor or they may call you Chief

But you're gonna have to serve somebody, yes indeed
You're gonna have to serve somebody
Well, it may be the devil or it may be the Lord
But you're gonna have to serve somebody

You may be a state trooper, you might be a young Turk
You may be the head of some big TV network
You may be rich or poor, you may be blind or lame
You may be living in another country under another name

But you're gonna have to serve somebody, yes indeed
You're gonna have to serve somebody
Well, it may be the devil or it may be the Lord
But you're gonna have to serve somebody

You may be a construction worker working on a home
You may be living in a mansion or you might live in a dome
You might own guns and you might even own tanks
You might be somebody's landlord, you might even own banks

But you're gonna have to serve somebody, yes indeed
You're gonna have to serve somebody
Well, it may be the devil or it may be the Lord
But you're gonna have to serve somebody

You may be a preacher with your spiritual pride
You may be a city councilman taking bribes on the side
You may be workin' in a barbershop, you may know how to cut hair
You may be somebody's mistress, may be somebody's heir

But you're gonna have to serve somebody, yes indeed
You're gonna have to serve somebody
Well, it may be the devil or it may be the Lord
But you're gonna have to serve somebody

Might like to wear cotton, might like to wear silk
Might like to drink whiskey, might like to drink milk
You might like to eat caviar, you might like to eat bread
You may be sleeping on the floor, sleeping in a king-sized bed

But you're gonna have to serve somebody, yes indeed
You're gonna have to serve somebody
Well, it may be the devil or it may be the Lord
But you're gonna have to serve somebody

You may call me Terry, you may call me Timmy
You may call me Bobby, you may call me Zimmy
You may call me R.J., you may call me Ray
You may call me anything but no matter what you say

You're gonna have to serve somebody, yes indeed
You're gonna have to serve somebody
Well, it may be the devil or it may be the Lord
But you're gonna have to serve somebody

心爱的天使

心爱的天使，日光之下
我怎么才能懂得你就是那个人
昭示我被蒙蔽，昭示我已离去
我所站立的根基多么脆弱？

如今兴起了属灵的争战，血肉崩解
你要么信要么不信，没有中立的地方
敌人狡猾，我们怎么如此受骗
当真相在我们心里，我们依然不信？

让你的光照耀，让你的光照耀我
让你的光照耀，让你的光照耀我
让你的光照耀，让你的光照耀我
你知道光靠我自己实在做不到
我过于盲目了些 [1]

我所谓的朋友已被迷住

1.《新约·哥林多后书》4:4："此等不信之人被这世界的神弄瞎了心眼，不叫
基督荣耀福音的光照着他们。"

他们直视着我的眼睛，他们说："一切都不赖"

他们可以想象将从高处坠落的黑暗吗

当人们祈求上帝杀死他们，他们却无法死去？

姐姐，让我告诉你我所看见的幻象

你在为丈夫汲水 [1]，你在律法之下受苦

你告诉他佛祖的事，同时你告诉他穆罕默德的事

你一次也未提及那个人，他到来，作为罪犯死去 [2]

让你的光照耀，让你的光照耀我

让你的光照耀，让你的光照耀我

让你的光照耀，让你的光照耀我

你知道光靠我自己实在做不到

我过于盲目了些

心爱的天使，你相信我，当我说

上帝赐予我们的，无人可以夺走

我们满身血腥，姑娘，你知道我们的先祖都是奴隶

让我们希望他们在尸骨累累的墓穴中找到了怜悯

1：《新约·约翰福音》4:7-18，耶稣在井旁与前来打水的撒玛利亚妇人交谈。
妇人有五个丈夫，却说自己没有丈夫，耶稣说："你现在有的，并不是你的丈夫，
你这话是真的。"
2. 指耶稣之死。

你是我肉身的女王，姑娘，你是我的女人，你是我的欢愉

你是我灵魂的羔羊，姑娘，你如火炬般照亮夜晚

但眼中带着狂热，姑娘，所以让我们抵住诱惑

在出埃及的路上，穿过埃塞俄比亚，来到基督的审判大厅

让你的光照耀，让你的光照耀我

让你的光照耀，让你的光照耀我

让你的光照耀，让你的光照耀我

你知道光靠我自己实在做不到

我过于盲目了些

Precious Angel

Precious angel, under the sun
How was I to know you'd be the one
To show me I was blinded, to show me I was gone
How weak was the foundation I was standing upon?

Now there's spiritual warfare and flesh and blood breaking
down
Ya either got faith or ya got unbelief and there ain't no
neutral ground
The enemy is subtle, how be it we are so deceived
When the truth's in our hearts and we still don't believe?

Shine your light, shine your light on me
Shine your light, shine your light on me
Shine your light, shine your light on me
Ya know I just couldn't make it by myself
I'm a little too blind to see

My so-called friends have fallen under a spell
They look me squarely in the eye and they say, "All is well"
Can they imagine the darkness that will fall from on high
When men will beg God to kill them and they won't be able
to die?

Sister, lemme tell you about a vision I saw
You were drawing water for your husband, you were suffering
under the law
You were telling him about Buddha, you were telling him
about Mohammed in the same breath

You never mentioned one time the Man who came and died
   a criminal's death

Shine your light, shine your light on me
Shine your light, shine your light on me
Shine your light, shine your light on me
Ya know I just couldn't make it by myself
I'm a little too blind to see

Precious angel, you believe me when I say
What God has given to us no man can take away
We are covered in blood, girl, you know our forefathers
   were slaves
Let us hope they've found mercy in their bone-filled graves

You're the queen of my flesh, girl, you're my woman, you're
   my delight
You're the lamp of my soul, girl, and you torch up the night
But there's violence in the eyes, girl, so let us not be enticed
On the way out of Egypt, through Ethiopia, to the judgment
   hall of Christ

Shine your light, shine your light on me
Shine your light, shine your light on me
Shine your light, shine your light on me
Ya know I just couldn't make it by myself
I'm a little too blind to see

我信任你

他们问我感觉如何
我的爱是否真心
我如何知道我可以熬过难关
他们，他们看着我，皱着眉头
他们想把我逐出这城镇
他们不想让我待在附近
因为我信任你

他们把我带到门口
他们说别再回来
因为我没有成为他们所希望的样子
我独自出走
离家千里
但我并不感到孤独
因为我信任你

我信任你，甚至通过眼泪和欢笑
我信任你，即使我们分离
我信任你，甚至在清晨过后
哦，当黄昏逼近

哦，当夜晚消隐

哦，这种感觉依然在这里，在我心里

别让我漂泊太远

让我待在你那里

在那里我一直可以得到新生

你今日给予我的东西

比我所能偿还的更有价值

无论他们说什么

我都信任你

我信任你，当冬天变成夏天

我信任你，当白变成黑

我信任你，即使我处于弱势

哦，即使大地会摇撼我

哦，即使朋友们都离弃我

哦，即使那样也不能使我回转

别让我变心

让我远离

他们所追逐的一切计划

我，我并不介意疼痛

并不介意倾盆大雨

我知道我会忍受
因为我信任你

I Believe in You

They ask me how I feel
And if my love is real
And how I know I'll make it through
And they, they look at me and frown
They'd like to drive me from this town
They don't want me around
'Cause I believe in you

They show me to the door
They say don't come back no more
'Cause I don't be like they'd like me to
And I walk out on my own
A thousand miles from home
But I don't feel alone
'Cause I believe in you

I believe in you even through the tears and the laughter
I believe in you even though we be apart
I believe in you even on the morning after
Oh, when the dawn is nearing
Oh, when the night is disappearing
Oh, this feeling is still here in my heart

Don't let me drift too far
Keep me where you are
Where I will always be renewed
And that which you've given me today
Is worth more than I could pay
And no matter what they say

I believe in you

I believe in you when winter turn to summer
I believe in you when white turn to black
I believe in you even though I be outnumbered
Oh, though the earth may shake me
Oh, though my friends forsake me
Oh, even that couldn't make me go back

Don't let me change my heart
Keep me set apart
From all the plans they do pursue
And I, I don't mind the pain
Don't mind the driving rain
I know I will sustain
'Cause I believe in you

慢车

有时候我感到如此卑微，令人厌恶
不禁想知道我的伙伴们发生了什么
他们迷失了吗，他们被找到了吗 [1]
他们计算过推翻世俗法则的代价吗
他们所有不得不抛弃的世俗法则？
有一列缓慢的、缓慢的火车正沿着弯道开来

我有一个女人在亚拉巴马州
她是一个乡下姑娘，但她的确很实在
她说："孩子，毫无疑问
得摆脱困境，回到正轨
不然你会死在这里，仅仅成为另一个事故的统计数据"
有一列缓慢的、缓慢的火车正沿着弯道开来

所有那些外国石油控制着美国国土
瞧瞧你四周，就必定让你局促不安
酋长们四处走动犹如帝王

1.《新约·路加福音》15，耶稣以寻回迷失的羊、失落的钱和浪子回家比喻
罪人悔改带来的欢喜。

戴着绮丽的珠宝和鼻环

从阿姆斯特丹到巴黎，决定着美国的未来

有一列缓慢的、缓慢的火车正沿着弯道开来

人的自我膨胀了，人的律法过时了，它们不再适用

你再不能只是站在旁边等着

在勇士的家乡

杰斐逊在坟墓里辗转不安

愚人们赞颂自己，试图操纵撒旦

有一列缓慢的、缓慢的火车正沿着弯道开来

精于谈判的高手、弄虚作假的术士和憎恨女人者

虚张声势的大师、出谋划策的大师

但我看见敌人

身披体面的斗篷

所有无信仰者和人贩子以宗教的名义在空谈

有一列缓慢的、缓慢的火车正沿着弯道开来

人们饥饿干渴，而谷仓满得都要爆裂

哦，你心知肚明，储存粮食的代价更高于施与

他们说松开你的禁制

跟从你的野心

他们谈论弟兄之爱的生活，告诉我有谁懂得这么生活

有一列缓慢的、缓慢的火车正沿着弯道开来

好吧，我的宝贝去了伊利诺伊，和某个她能毁掉的脏话
　　男孩
一场真正的自杀事件，但我做什么也阻止不了
我不在乎经济
我不在乎天文
但看见那些我心爱的人变成木偶，的确让我烦忧
有一列缓慢的、缓慢的火车正沿着弯道开来

Slow Train

Sometimes I feel so low-down and disgusted
Can't help but wonder what's happenin' to my companions
Are they lost or are they found
Have they counted the cost it'll take to bring down
All their earthly principles they're gonna have to abandon?
There's a slow, slow train comin' up around the bend

I had a woman down in Alabama
She was a backwoods girl, but she sure was realistic
She said, "Boy, without a doubt
Have to quit your mess and straighten out
You could die down here, be just another accident statistic"
There's a slow, slow train comin' up around the bend

All that foreign oil controlling American soil
Look around you, it's just bound to make you embarrassed
Sheiks walkin' around like kings
Wearing fancy jewels and nose rings
Deciding America's future from Amsterdam and to Paris
And there's a slow, slow train comin' up around the bend

Man's ego is inflated, his laws are outdated, they don't apply
    no more
You can't rely no more to be standin' around waitin'
In the home of the brave
Jefferson turnin' over in his grave
Fools glorifying themselves, trying to manipulate Satan
And there's a slow, slow train comin' up around the bend

Big-time negotiators, false healers and woman haters
Masters of the bluff and masters of the proposition
But the enemy I see
Wears a cloak of decency
All nonbelievers and men stealers talkin' in the name of religion
And there's a slow, slow train comin' up around the bend

People starving and thirsting, grain elevators are bursting
Oh, you know it costs more to store the food than it do to give it
They say lose your inhibitions
Follow your own ambitions
They talk about a life of brotherly love show me someone who knows how to live it
There's a slow, slow train comin' up around the bend

Well, my baby went to Illinois with some bad-talkin' boy she could destroy
A real suicide case, but there was nothin' I could do to stop it
I don't care about economy
I don't care about astronomy
But it sure do bother me to see my loved ones turning into puppets
There's a slow, slow train comin' up around the bend

要变换我的思考方式

要变换我的思考方式
为我自己制定一套不同的规则
要变换我的思考方式
为我自己制定一套不同的规则
要迈出好的一步
不再受愚人影响

这么多压迫
不能再记录
这么多压迫
不能再记录
儿子成为自己母亲的丈夫
老男人把年轻的女儿们变成妓女

你肩上的鞭痕 [1]
你背上、你手上的鞭痕
你肩上的鞭痕
你背上、你手上的鞭痕

1.《新约·马太福音》27:26,被捕的耶稣受鞭打。

刀剑刺穿你的肋旁

血和水流过大地 [1]

嗯，我们不知道何者更糟糕

我行我素，或只是冷漠

嗯，我们不知道何者更糟糕

我行我素，或只是冷漠

你只惦记着黄铜铃 [2]

你全忘了黄金律 [3]

你可以误导一个男人

你可以用你的双眼攫住他的心

你可以误导一个男人

你可以用你的双眼攫住他的心

然而只存在一个权柄

那是在天上的权柄

我有了个敬畏上帝的女人

1.《新约·约翰福音》19:34："惟有一个兵拿枪扎他（耶稣）的肋旁，随即有血和水流出来。"

2. 黄铜铃，俚语指能致发迹、成功的机遇。

3. 黄金律，指《新约·马太福音》7:12，耶稣说"无论何事，你们愿意人怎样待你们，你们也要怎样待人"。

我可以毫不费力地养活她

我有了个敬畏上帝的女人

我可以毫不费力地养活她

她可以跳佐治亚州舞 [1]

她可以靠主的灵行事 [2]

耶稣说过："要预备

因为你不知道我在哪一个时辰到来"

耶稣说过："要预备

因为你不知道我在哪一个时辰到来"

他说过："不与我相合的就是敌我的"

所以你知道他来自何处

有一个王国叫作天堂

这个地方没有生育的疼痛 [3]

有一个王国叫作天堂

这个地方没有生育的疼痛

嗯，上帝创造了它，先生

同时创造了尘世

---

1. 20 世纪初源自美国佐治亚州的一种蓝调伴奏舞蹈，舞姿多带性意味。

2.《新约·加拉太书》5:25："我们若是靠圣灵得生，就当靠圣灵行事。"

3.《旧约·创世记》3:16，人类堕落后，上帝对夏娃说"我必多多增加你怀胎的苦楚，你生产儿女必多受苦楚"。《新约·启示录》21:4，提到"新天新地"中不再有疼痛。

Gonna Change My Way of Thinking

Gonna change my way of thinking
Make myself a different set of rules
Gonna change my way of thinking
Make myself a different set of rules
Gonna put my good foot forward
And stop being influenced by fools

So much oppression
Can't keep track of it no more
So much oppression
Can't keep track of it no more
Sons becoming husbands to their mothers
And old men turning young daughters into whores

Stripes on your shoulders
Stripes on your back and on your hands
Stripes on your shoulders
Stripes on your back and on your hands
Swords piercing your side
Blood and water flowing through the land

Well don't know which one is worse
Doing your own thing or just being cool
Well don't know which one is worse
Doing your own thing or just being cool
You remember only about the brass ring
You forget all about the golden rule

You can mislead a man

You can take ahold of his heart with your eyes
You can mislead a man
You can take ahold of his heart with your eyes
But there's only one authority
And that's the authority on high

I got a God-fearing woman
One I can easily afford
I got a God-fearing woman
One I can easily afford
She can do the Georgia crawl
She can walk in the spirit of the Lord

Jesus said, "Be ready
For you know not the hour in which I come"
Jesus said, "Be ready
For you know not the hour in which I come"
He said, "He who is not for Me is against Me"
Just so you know where He's coming from

There's a kingdom called Heaven
A place where there is no pain of birth
There's a kingdom called Heaven
A place where there is no pain of birth
Well the Lord created it, mister
About the same time He made the earth

要变换我的思考方式
（另一版本）

变换我的思考方式，为我自己制定一套不同的规则

变换我的思考方式，为我自己制定一套不同的规则

迈出好的一步，不再受愚人影响

我坐在迎接席旁，我饿得可以吃下一匹马

我坐在迎接席旁，我饿得可以吃下一匹马

我要让自己的思想复苏，我要让律法运行如常

耶稣在召唤，他正回来集起珍宝

耶稣在召唤，他正回来集起珍宝

只要取得了黄金律，我们就生活于黄金律下

阳光照耀，只不过是一辆轨道上的火车

阳光照耀，只不过是一辆轨道上的火车

我正步出黑暗森林，我正跳上猴子的背

我穿好盛装，要去县里的舞会

我穿好盛装，要去县里的舞会

每一天你想要祈求指引
每一天你想要给自己一个机会

风暴在海上，风暴也在山上
风暴在海上，风暴也在山上
主啊，你知道我没有像你一样的朋友

我会告诉你一些事情，这事情你从未拥有，永不失去
我会告诉你一些事情，这事情你从未拥有，永不失去
勇士用剑杀你，胆小鬼则用吻

Gonna Change My Way of Thinking
(Alternate Version)

Change my way of thinking, make myself a different set of
    rules
Change my way of thinking, make myself a different set of
    rules
Put my best foot forward, stop being influenced by fools

I'm sittin' at the welcome table, I'm so hungry I could eat a
    horse
I'm sittin' at the welcome table, I'm so hungry I could eat a
    horse
I'm gonna revitalize my thinking, I'm gonna let the law take
    its course

Jesus is calling, He's coming back to gather up his jewels
Jesus is calling, He's coming back to gather up his jewels
We living by the golden rule, whoever got the gold rules

The sun is shining, ain't but one train on this track
The sun is shining, ain't but one train on this track
I'm stepping out of the dark woods, I'm jumping on the
    monkey's back

I'm all dressed up, I'm going to the county dance
I'm all dressed up, I'm going to the county dance
Every day you got to pray for guidance
Every day you got to give yourself a chance

Storms are on the ocean, storms out on the mountain, too
Storms are on the ocean, storms out on the mountain, too
Oh Lord, you know I have no friend like you

I'll tell you something, things you never had you'll never
    miss
I'll tell you something, things you never had you'll never
    miss
A brave man will kill you with a sword, a coward with a kiss

好好待我，宝贝
（待别人）

不想论断什么人，不想被论断

不想触摸什么人，不想被触摸

不想伤害什么人，不想被伤害

不想对待什么人如同污泥

但你若好好待我，宝贝

我也会好好待你

你要待别人

就像你想要他们，就像你想要他们，如何待你

不想枪击什么人，不想被枪击

不想收买什么人，不想被收买

不想埋葬什么人，不想被埋葬

不想与什么人结婚，倘若他们已婚

但你若好好待我，宝贝

我也会好好待你

你要待别人

就像你想要他们，就像你想要他们，如何待你

不想焚烧什么人，不想被焚烧

不想从什么人那里学习我要抛却的东西

不想欺骗什么人，不想被骗

不想击败什么人，倘若他们已落败

但你若好好待我，宝贝

我也会好好待你

你要待别人

就像你想要他们，就像你想要他们，如何待你

不想向什么人挤眼，不想被挤眼相向 ¹

不想为了一块门垫被人利用

不想迷惑什么人，不想被迷惑

不想逗乐什么人，不想被逗乐

但你若好好待我，宝贝

我也会好好待你

你要待别人

就像你想要他们，就像你想要他们，如何待你

1.《旧约·诗篇》35:19："不容那无故恨我的向我挤眼。"

不想背叛什么人，不想被背叛

不想与什么人嬉戏，不想被伏击

不想惦念什么人，不想被惦念

不要相信什么人，即便科学家也不行

但你若好好待我，宝贝

我也会好好待你

你要待别人

就像你想要他们，就像你想要他们，如何待你

Do Right to Me Baby
(Do Unto Others)

Don't wanna judge nobody, don't wanna be judged
Don't wanna touch nobody, don't wanna be touched
Don't wanna hurt nobody, don't wanna be hurt
Don't wanna treat nobody like they was dirt

But if you do right to me, baby
I'll do right to you, too
Ya got to do unto others
Like you'd have them, like you'd have them, do unto you

Don't wanna shoot nobody, don't wanna be shot
Don't wanna buy nobody, don't wanna be bought
Don't wanna bury nobody, don't wanna be buried
Don't wanna marry nobody if they're already married

But if you do right to me, baby
I'll do right to you, too
Ya got to do unto others
Like you'd have them, like you'd have them, do unto you

Don't wanna burn nobody, don't wanna be burned
Don't wanna learn from nobody what I gotta unlearn
Don't wanna cheat nobody, don't wanna be cheated
Don't wanna defeat nobody if they already been defeated

But if you do right to me, baby
I'll do right to you, too

Ya got to do unto others
Like you'd have them, like you'd have them, do unto you

Don't wanna wink at nobody, don't wanna be winked at
Don't wanna be used by nobody for a doormat
Don't wanna confuse nobody, don't wanna be confused
Don't wanna amuse nobody, don't wanna be amused

But if you do right to me, baby
I'll do right to you, too
Ya got to do unto others
Like you'd have them, like you'd have them, do unto you

Don't wanna betray nobody, don't wanna be betrayed
Don't wanna play with nobody, don't wanna be waylaid
Don't wanna miss nobody, don't wanna be missed
Don't put my faith in nobody, not even a scientist

But if you do right to me, baby
I'll do right to you, too
Ya got to do unto others
Like you'd have them, like you'd have them, do unto you

人命名了所有动物

人命名了所有动物
在起初，在起初
人命名了所有动物
在起初，很久以前

他看见一只动物喜欢咆哮
毛茸茸的大爪子，它喜欢嚎叫
巨大的毛茸茸的背，毛茸茸的毛发
"啊，我想我会叫它熊"

人命名了所有动物
在起初，在起初
人命名了所有动物
在起初，很久以前

他看见一只动物在山上
咀嚼那么多草，直到它填饱肚子
他看见奶流出来，但他不知道如何流出来
"啊，我想我会叫它奶牛"

人命名了所有动物

在起初，在起初

人命名了所有动物

在起初，很久以前

他看见一只动物喜欢喷响鼻

它头上有角，而且不太短

看起来好像没有什么它拉不动

"啊，我想我会叫它公牛"

人命名了所有动物

在起初，在起初

人命名了所有动物

在起初，很久以前

他看见一只动物留下了泥泞的足迹

肮脏不堪的脸，一条卷曲的尾巴

它不太小也不太大

"啊，我想我会叫它猪"

人命名了所有动物

在起初，在起初

人命名了所有动物

在起初，很久以前

下一只他所遇见的动物
背上长着毛，脚上长着蹄
在那么陡峭的山坡上吃草
"啊，我想我会叫它羊"

人命名了所有动物
在起初，在起初
人命名了所有动物
在起初，很久以前

他看见一只动物像玻璃一样光滑
它滑行着，穿过草丛
看见它消失在湖边的一棵树旁……[1]

---

1. 暗指《旧约·创世记》3:1-4 中，在伊甸园里诱惑人类吃禁果的蛇。

Man Gave Names to All the Animals

Man gave names to all the animals
In the beginning, in the beginning
Man gave names to all the animals
In the beginning, long time ago

He saw an animal that liked to growl
Big furry paws and he liked to howl
Great big furry back and furry hair
"Ah, think I'll call it a bear"

Man gave names to all the animals
In the beginning, in the beginning
Man gave names to all the animals
In the beginning, long time ago

He saw an animal up on a hill
Chewing up so much grass until she was filled
He saw milk comin' out but he didn't know how
"Ah, think I'll call it a cow"

Man gave names to all the animals
In the beginning, in the beginning
Man gave names to all the animals
In the beginning, long time ago

He saw an animal that liked to snort
Horns on his head and they weren't too short
It looked like there wasn't nothin' that he couldn't pull
"Ah, think I'll call it a bull"

Man gave names to all the animals
In the beginning, in the beginning
Man gave names to all the animals
In the beginning, long time ago

He saw an animal leavin' a muddy trail
Real dirty face and a curly tail
He wasn't too small and he wasn't too big
"Ah, think I'll call it a pig"

Man gave names to all the animals
In the beginning, in the beginning
Man gave names to all the animals
In the beginning, long time ago

Next animal that he did meet
Had wool on his back and hooves on his feet
Eating grass on a mountainside so steep
"Ah, think I'll call it a sheep"

Man gave names to all the animals
In the beginning, in the beginning
Man gave names to all the animals
In the beginning, long time ago

He saw an animal as smooth as glass
Slithering his way through the grass
Saw him disappear by a tree near a lake…

当他归来

铁腕不是铁杖[1]的对手

最坚固的墙会在一个有大能的神前崩塌

对于所有生有眼睛和所有生有耳朵的人

只有他能使我落泪

你不要哭泣，你不要死去，你不要燃烧

因为在夜里，像个盗贼[2]，他会用对代替错

当他归来

真理是箭，它穿过的门是窄的

他在无人知晓的未知时刻释放了自己的力量

我能倾听偏见的谎言多久？

我能在旷野的恐惧中喝醉多久？

我可以抛开吗，这所有的忠诚和骄傲？

我会知道，不会有和平，战争不会停止

直到他归来吗？

在这血染的土地上，交出你的王冠，摘下你的面具

---

1. 铁杖，《新约·启示录》2:27，提到耶稣"必用铁杖辖管他们"。
2.《新约·帖撒罗尼迦前书》5:2："主的日子来到，好像夜间的贼一样。"

他察看你的行为，他知道你所需用的，甚至在你祈求

以先 [1]

你能歪曲并否认真实的事物多久？

你能为自己隐藏的弱点而恨自己多久？

对于每一个人所皆知的尘世计划，他不关心

他有自己的计划来设立他的王位

当他归来

1.《新约·马太福音》6:8，耶稣说：“你们不可效法他们（外邦人），因为你们没有祈求以先，你们所需用的，你们的父早已知道了。”

When He Returns

The iron hand it ain't no match for the iron rod
The strongest wall will crumble and fall to a mighty God
For all those who have eyes and all those who have ears
It is only He who can reduce me to tears
Don't you cry and don't you die and don't you burn
For like a thief in the night, He'll replace wrong with right
When He returns

Truth is an arrow and the gate is narrow that it passes through
He unleashed His power at an unknown hour that no one
    knew
How long can I listen to the lies of prejudice?
How long can I stay drunk on fear out in the wilderness?
Can I cast it aside, all this loyalty and this pride?
Will I ever learn that there'll be no peace, that the war won't
    cease
Until He returns?

Surrender your crown on this blood-stained ground, take
    off your mask
He sees your deeds, He knows your needs even before you
    ask
How long can you falsify and deny what is real?
How long can you hate yourself for the weakness you
    conceal?
Of every earthly plan that be known to man, He is
    unconcerned
He's got plans of His own to set up His throne
When He returns

没有义人，对，一个也没有 [1]

当一个人侍奉上帝，这让他的生命有了价值
他的立场不要紧，他的生活方式不要紧
说起完美，我一次也没见过
没有义人，对，一个也没有

有时候魔鬼喜欢把你从邻居身边赶走
他甚至会通过那些善良用心的人来得逞
有些人喜欢对月亮崇拜，别的人在崇拜太阳
没有义人，对，一个也没有

环顾四周，你看到很多社会上的伪君子
喜欢为别人制订规则，而自己的行为恰恰相反

你不能通过升起或降下什么旗帜来获得荣耀
把你的仁慈挨着上帝的，它就变得像污秽的衣服 [2]
在黑暗的城市里不需要阳光

1.《新约·罗马书》3:10 ："就如经上所记：'没有义人，连一个也没有……'"
2.《旧约·以赛亚书》64:6 ："我们都像不洁净的人，所有的义都像污秽的衣服……"

没有义人，对，一个也没有

以爱的名义做了那么多邪恶的事，这太可耻
我从未见过能扑灭火焰的火

拉下你的帽子，宝贝，蒙住你的眼睛
继续扯，宝贝，直到你用尽了借口
总有一天你会为你所做的一切负责
嗯，没有义人，对，一个也没有

上帝有力量，人有他的虚妄
人要作出选择，在上帝让他自由之前
你不知道日光之下并无新事吗？
嗯，没有义人，对，一个也没有

当我离开，不要疑惑我会在哪里
只要说我信靠神，基督就在我心里
说他打败了魔鬼，他是上帝选定的儿子
没有义人，对，一个也没有

Ain't No Man Righteous, No Not One

When a man he serves the Lord, it makes his life worthwhile
It don't matter 'bout his position, it don't matter 'bout his
   lifestyle
Talk about perfection, I ain't never seen none
And there ain't no man righteous, no not one

Sometimes the devil likes to drive you from the neighborhood
He'll even work his ways through those whose intentions are
   good
Some like to worship on the moon, others are worshipping
   the sun
And there ain't no man righteous, no not one

Look around, ya see so many social hypocrites
Like to make rules for others while they do just the opposite

You can't get to glory by the raising and the lowering of no
   flag
Put your goodness next to God's and it comes out like a
   filthy rag
In a city of darkness there's no need of the sun
And there ain't no man righteous, no not one

Done so many evil things in the name of love, it's a crying
   shame
I never did see no fire that could put out a flame

Pull your hat down, baby, pull the wool down over your
   eyes

Keep a-talking, baby, 'til you run right out of alibis
Someday you'll account for all the deeds that you done
Well, there ain't no man righteous, no not one

God got the power, man has got his vanity
Man gotta choose before God can set him free
Don't you know there's nothing new that's under the sun?
Well, there ain't no man righteous, no not one

When I'm gone don't wonder where I be
Just say that I trusted in God and that Christ was in me
Say He defeated the devil, He was God's chosen Son
And that there ain't no man righteous, no not one

烦恼在心中

我知道了，主啊，当勒住缰绳时
死亡便可能由最受低估的痛苦所致
撒旦低声对你说："好吧，我不想惹你烦
但当你对某某小姐厌倦了，我就给你别的女人"

烦恼在心中，主啊，烦恼在心中
主啊，将这心中的烦恼带走

当你做的事情没有总计归零
内在的东西才算数，问问任何战争英雄
你以为你能够隐藏，但你永远不是独自一人
问问罗得怎么想，当他妻子变成石头 [1]

烦恼在心中，主啊，烦恼在心中
主啊，将这心中的烦恼带走

撒旦来了，空中掌权者的首领

1.《旧约·创世记》19:26，罗得一家在天使指引下逃出毁灭在即的所多玛，
城毁时，"罗得的妻子在后边回头一看，就变成了一根盐柱"。

他会为你制定自己的律法，在你发间造一个鸟巢

他会使你的良知麻木，你跪拜自己手所造的 [1]

你将服务于外邦人，在一片陌生的、被遗弃的土地

烦恼在心中，主啊，烦恼在心中

主啊，将这心中的烦恼带走

好吧，你的真爱逮住了你，在非你所属的地方

你说："宝贝，每个人都这么做，所以我猜这不会错"

真理在远离你的地方，所以你知道你必须撒谎

然后你一直在捍卫你永远无法辩护的事情

烦恼在心中，主啊，烦恼在心中

主啊，将这心中的烦恼带走

我的那么多兄弟，他们仍然想当老板

他们不能与天国联系在一起，不能与十字架联系在一起

他们对自己破碎的生命施以自我惩罚

将信仰寄托在财产上，寄托在工作或妻子上

1.《旧约·以赛亚书》2:8："他们的地满了偶像，他们跪拜自己手所造的，就是自己指头所作的。"

烦恼在心中，主啊，烦恼在心中
主啊，将这心中的烦恼带走

当我的生命结束，它会像一阵轻烟
我必须忍受多久，主啊，我必须被激怒多久？
撒旦会给你一点甜头，然后迅速侵入
主啊，遮挡我盲目的一面，确保我不会流血

Trouble in Mind

I got to know, Lord, when to pull back on the reins
Death can be the result of the most underrated pain
Satan whispers to ya, "Well, I don't want to bore ya
But when ya get tired of the Miss So-and-so I got another
   woman for ya"

Trouble in mind, Lord, trouble in mind
Lord, take away this trouble in mind

When the deeds that you do don't add up to zero
It's what's inside that counts, ask any war hero
You think you can hide but you're never alone
Ask Lot what he thought when his wife turned to stone

Trouble in mind, Lord, trouble in mind
Lord, take away this trouble in mind

Here comes Satan, prince of the power of the air
He's gonna make you a law unto yourself, gonna build a
   bird's nest in your hair
He's gonna deaden your conscience 'til you worship the
   work of your own hands
You'll be serving strangers in a strange, forsaken land

Trouble in mind, Lord, trouble in mind
Lord, take away this trouble in mind

Well, your true love has caught you where you don't belong

You say, "Baby, everybody's doing it so I guess it can't be
   wrong"
The truth is far from you, so you know you got to lie
Then you're all the time defending what you can never
   justify

Trouble in mind, Lord, trouble in mind
Lord, take away this trouble in mind

So many of my brothers, they still want to be the boss
They can't relate to the Lord's kingdom, they can't relate to
   the cross
They self-inflict punishment on their own broken lives
Put their faith in their possessions, in their jobs or their
   wives

Trouble in mind, Lord, trouble in mind
Lord, take away this trouble in mind

When my life is over, it'll be like a puff of smoke
How long must I suffer, Lord, how long must I be
   provoked?
Satan will give you a little taste, then he'll move in with
   rapid speed
Lord, keep my blind side covered and see that I don't bleed

你要改变

你积蓄怒气
你知道没有太多的刺激
你渴求满足
但你的空虚无法被填满
你已拥有了足够的仇恨
你的骨头在破碎，发觉不了神圣的东西

你要改变，你要改变
眨眼之间，当最后的号筒吹响
死者将复活，冲破你的衣服
你也要改变 [1]

你既得的一切
凭着汗水、血和肌肉而得
从清晨直到黑暗降临
你所做的一切只是奔忙
所有你爱的人都走出了门

---

1. 以上三行歌词源自《新约·哥林多前书》15:52："眨眼之间，号筒末次吹响的时候；因号筒要响，死人要复活，成为不朽坏的，我们也要改变。"

你甚至不再对你的妻子和孩子深信不疑，但

你要改变，你要改变
眨眼之间，当最后的号筒吹响
死者将复活，冲破你的衣服
你也要改变

过去不能控制你
但未来就像赌博轮盘一样旋转
在内心深处
你知道你需要一个全新的开始
不必去俄罗斯或伊朗
只要向上帝投降，他会就在你站立之处改变你，而

你要改变，你要改变
眨眼之间，当最后的号筒吹响
死者将复活，冲破你的衣服
你也要改变

你饮苦水 [1]

1.《旧约·出埃及记》15:23：摩西带领以色列人穿越旷野，找不到水，"到了玛拉，不能喝那里的水，因为水是苦的……"

你一直吃着愁苦的饭 [1]

你不能为今日而活

当你心里永远思虑着明天

你跋涉的道路一直崎岖不平

当你觉得已经受够了，那么

你要改变，你要改变

眨眼之间，当最后的号筒吹响

死者将复活，冲破你的衣服

你也要改变

1.《旧约·诗篇》127:2："你们早起、晚睡、吃愁苦的饭，本是虚空。"

Ye Shall Be Changed

You harbor resentment
You know there ain't too much of a thrill
You wish for contentment
But you got an emptiness that can't be filled
You've had enough of hatred
Your bones are breaking, can't find nothing sacred

Ye shall be changed, ye shall be changed
In a twinkling of an eye, when the last trumpet blows
The dead will arise and burst out of your clothes
And ye shall be changed

Everything you've gotten
You've gotten by sweat, blood and muscle
From early in the morning 'til way past dark
All you ever do is hustle
All your loved ones have walked out the door
You're not even sure 'bout your wife and kids no more, but

Ye shall be changed, ye shall be changed
In a twinkling of an eye, when the last trumpet blows
The dead will arise and burst out of your clothes
And ye shall be changed

The past don't control you
But the future's like a roulette wheel spinning
Deep down inside
You know you need a whole new beginning
Don't have to go to Russia or Iran

Just surrender to God and He'll move you right here where
   you stand, and

Ye shall be changed, ye shall be changed
In a twinkling of an eye, when the last trumpet blows
The dead will arise and burst out of your clothes
And ye shall be changed

You drink bitter water
And you been eating the bread of sorrow
You can't live for today
When all you're ever thinking of is tomorrow
The path you've endured has been rough
When you've decided that you've had enough, then

Ye shall be changed, ye shall be changed
In a twinkling of an eye, when the last trumpet blows
The dead will arise and burst out of your clothes
And ye shall be changed